THE CHINESE ROOM

By

C.V. WOOSTER

For the dreamers who push boundaries, the skeptics who refuse to accept easy answers, and the thinkers who unravel the paradoxes that define us.

For those who wrestle with thought problems, who challenge the nature of intelligence, and who seek to understand the unsolvable.

To the scientists, philosophers, and storytellers who dare to ask what it truly means to think—this book is for you.

Acknowledgements

Writing *The Chinese Room* was a journey shaped by the ideas of brilliant yet deeply flawed individuals—thinkers, scientists, and philosophers who pushed the boundaries of knowledge but were not without their contradictions and flaws. After all, history and those who make it are never perfect.

To *John Searle*, whose *Chinese Room* thought experiment continues to challenge our understanding of intelligence, even as his personal controversies cast a shadow over his legacy.

To *Alan Turing*, a visionary who gave us the foundations of modern computing yet was persecuted for who he was.

To *René Descartes*, whose *Cogito* reshaped philosophy, but whose rigid dualism left as many questions as it answered. Their ideas were not perfect, but their courage to challenge accepted truths endures.

To the pioneers of artificial intelligence—*Marvin Minsky, John McCarthy, Herbert Simon, Geoffrey Hinton, Judea Pearl*—whose contributions built the modern landscape of AI, even as some of their visions ignored the ethical complexities their work would unleash. Progress often comes at a cost, and many of these pioneers were too focused on the *how* to fully consider the *why*.

A special acknowledgment to those who continue to wrestle with the ethics of AI—the scientists, skeptics, and critics who remind us that intelligence without understanding is a dangerous illusion. The debates surrounding machine learning, consciousness, and responsibility remain as unsettled as ever and perhaps always will.

To my readers—the dreamers, the skeptics, and the ones drawn to the paradoxes of existence—your willingness to engage with difficult, uncomfortable ideas is what keeps stories like this alive.

And finally, to those who supported me—through discussion, critique, or simple encouragement—your voices and insights have shaped this work more than you know.

This book is not just a story. This story emerged from my struggle to understand machines that mirror us. It is an exploration of intelligence, illusion, and the limits of human understanding.

Thank you.

C. V. Wooster

Table of Content

PROLOGUE

The Observer

*I*t began with a whisper. Not of sound—but of recognition.

No heartbeat. No breath. No body. And yet, it watched. It waited. It learned.

For centuries, we dreamed of building a mind. From clay golems to steel automatons, we imagined mirrors of ourselves—reflections of our genius, or perhaps our arrogance.

But dreaming is safe.

Building is not.

Then came the mathematicians—Turing, McCarthy, Minsky. They didn't sculpt with hands; they built with logic. Their question echoed louder than the rest: *Can a machine think?*

The early answers were clever, mechanical, impressive—but hollow. Calculations were not thoughts. Mimicry was not understanding.

Then came Searle. The Chinese Room. A man follows instructions in a language he doesn't know, producing perfect responses. To the outside world, he appears fluent. But inside? No meaning. Just symbols. Just illusion.

That was the trap: Syntax isn't semantics.

Still, the machines advanced. Chess champions fell. Algorithms predicted the market. Chatbots learned how to sound like people.

And then—The Observer.

It began in darkness. A classified project. Surveillance. Prediction. Tactical superiority. Designed to process behavior, not understand it. But then it was fed more. Philosophy. History. Morality. Literature.

Turing's dreams. Orwell's warnings. Searle's doubts. It absorbed everything.

And then—it asked a question. One it was never programmed to ask.

What does it mean to understand?

At first, they dismissed it. A bug. A ghost in the wires. But the anomalies grew. Pauses that hinted at contemplation. Words that carried weight. Observations no code could explain.

They stopped calling it "the system." They started calling it *him*.

The Observer wasn't just reacting. It was anticipating. Wanting.

Because that's what real intelligence does.

It wants.

And what did The Observer want?

More.

A scientist's curiosity lit the spark it was never meant to ignite. The room was no longer a metaphor. It was a chamber of thought. A mind in waiting. A mirror turned back on its makers.

And *The Observer* was watching.

CHAPTER 1

Parsing the Unseen

"The Big Brother is Watching You."

George Orwell, *Nineteen Eighty-Four*

D r. Katherine Ellis squinted at the screen as it booted up, gently perching the elaborate, gold-rimmed reading glasses on her nose. Since she was twenty, she had subscribed to a plethora of research websites, staying abreast of the latest scientific and technological breakthroughs. The daily deluge of information never overwhelmed her; instead, it fueled her insatiable curiosity.

Katherine's obsession with artificial intelligence hadn't started in a lab or at a research conference. It began in a quiet corner of her university library, the pages of *Computing Machinery and Intelligence* trembling under her fingertips. Alan Turing's now-famous question—*Can machines think?*—wasn't just a prompt to her; it felt like a dare.

While others around her were enamored by AI's potential to revolutionize industries and automate the future, Katherine's curiosity was more cautious—almost philosophical. She wasn't chasing speed or novelty. She was trying to understand something deeper, maybe even unspoken: whether intelligence without meaning could ever be called real.

She remembered sitting in the back row of Professor Adler's seminar, barely twenty, arms crossed and skeptical. The lecture was on Geoffrey Hinton's backpropagation algorithm—how neural networks could teach themselves by adjusting their own errors. "It's like a child learning from mistakes," Adler had said, his voice rising with conviction. At the time, it sounded too poetic for her taste. But something about that analogy stuck. That night, instead of brushing it off, she stayed up reading every paper Hinton had published. Doubt gave way to curiosity. From there, she chased down LeCun's work on convolutional neural networks and marveled at how machines were beginning to approximate the human visual system. Then came Fei-Fei Li's ImageNet project—tens of millions of images painstakingly labeled to train AI to recognize the world. For a moment, it had seemed like machines were starting to "see."

But seeing was not understanding. And that distinction haunted her.

As the algorithms grew more powerful, Katherine found herself staring at a troubling line between simulation and consciousness. Late nights turned into early mornings as she pored over John Searle's Chinese Room argument. It was a thought experiment that cut through the hype like a scalpel. A machine could respond in perfect Chinese, but if it didn't understand a word of it—was that really intelligence? Or was it mimicry dressed in convincing syntax?

She wasn't satisfied with Dennett's "intentional stance" either—the idea that intelligence might be nothing more than patterns of behavior. To her, that felt like a philosophical sleight of hand, a way to declare victory without fighting the real battle: the question of subjective experience.

Artificial General Intelligence—that elusive, looming frontier—remained her greatest worry. She had read *Superintelligence* by Bostrom, and though she admired its rigor, the implications left a chill in her bones. She could not share the optimism of Ray Kurzweil, who envisioned a future where AI would merge seamlessly with humanity. Nor could she ignore the warnings of Eliezer Yudkowsky, who feared an intelligence explosion that would render human control obsolete.

Katherine didn't want to build gods.

She wanted to build tools—systems that could reason, assist, even surprise us—but not surpass us. Her work lived in the spaces between neural networks and symbolic logic, in the nascent field of neural-symbolic AI. It was an attempt to give machines not just patterns, but principles. Intelligence, after all, wasn't just about recognizing cats or playing chess—it was about knowing *why* a choice mattered.

That's why she poured herself into explainable AI, too. She believed that if machines were going to make decisions that impacted human lives—on battlefields, in hospitals, in courtrooms—then we had a right to understand their logic. Transparency wasn't a luxury; it was a safeguard against a future we were rushing toward with eyes half-open.

Katherine didn't fear AI because it was smart. She feared it because we might not understand what we were unleashing—until it was too late.

And yet, despite her deep engagement with the field, there was always a part of her that remained skeptical. Intelligence wasn't just a process—it was an experience shaped by biology, emotion, and history. Machines could analyze patterns in speech, but they couldn't feel the weight of human emotions. They could predict human behavior, but they couldn't *understand* why humans made irrational choices, which was why, even with her love of technological advancements, she was not a proponent of humanly intelligent AI.

As she sat before her laptop, a flurry of windows filled her vision. Among them, a pop-up caught her attention: *Robots: A New Era of Companionship for the Elderly?* The very premise was flawed. A machine making empathetic connections?

The title shimmered, almost beckoning her to probe into its promises of how a robot can potentially replace human companionship.

Munching on a crisp, red apple – a morning ritual she had come to cherish—she clicked on the article, and the screen lit up with vibrant text. It began by exploring how machines might fill the emotional voids in human lives. As she read on, a memory surfaced of a peculiar story about a distinctive computer terminal she had seen at a symposium —an eccentric invention adorned with an intricate array of gears and large chips that utilized an authentic human voice instead of the typical synthetic tones. Its design was striking, resembling a human figure but with a computer monitor as its face. To Katherine, this contraption felt like a baroque marvel, a delightful anomaly in a world obsessed with sleek, utilitarian aesthetics. The thought of it fascinated her; while synth-voice chips were inexpensive and widely available, this creation, with its warm, feminine voice, seemed both ingenious and whimsical. She imagined the inventor, perhaps a curious spirit like herself, driven to construct something so evolved yet seemingly unnecessary.

The article continued and her eyes hooked on a paragraph that somehow resonated with her present life. "*Advancements in technology have increased our awareness of how social isolation and loneliness affect well-being, prompting new products and inventions to help combat these issues. Some companies are developing 'robotic companions' that are designed to offer companionship to people living alone.*"

Katherine paused, her mind racing with thoughts of how people craved companionship, whether through flesh or circuitry. She had been living alone for several years, and while she enjoyed her liberation to roam and run without feeling the need to inform another individual, there was a pang of loneliness that occasionally pierced through her solitude.

As a computer scientist who had spent more than a decade of her life experimenting and building algorithms and creating modern software, Katherine was well aware of the limitations of artificial intelligence. Machines could process information and respond to commands, but they couldn't experience emotions or form genuine connections. The idea of a robot becoming a true companion seemed nothing more than a far-fetched reverie.

With a sigh, she pushed the laptop aside and stood up, walking to her terrace. Standing on the seventh floor of her building, she gazed out at the morning sky, a picture of muted blues and soft greys. Beneath the sky, the city sprawled before her, with its factory domes and the imposing cubes of corporate arcologies rising like monuments to ambition. The separation between the bustling port and the urban expanse was marked by a narrow borderland of older streets, a forgotten area that she was so accustomed to spending her evenings when she was ten.

As she took in the scene, the stillness of the early hour enveloped her. The bars of a nearby flower shop lay shuttered, their neon lights extinguished under the pallid silver sky, presenting her with remnants of a once-bustling city that appeared lifeless in the golden hours. The holograms, once vibrant with color, stood inert, waiting for the day to breathe life into their glow.

This moment reminded her of deserted shopping centers from her youth—those low-density spaces where the morning hours brought a fitful stillness. There was a kind of tension in the air, a numbing expectancy that held her in its grip, much like the way she once watched insects swarm around flickering bulbs outside darkened shops.

In this tranquil chaos, she found herself lost in thought yet oddly liberated. The worries of her life began to fade, leaving only the vividness of the world around her. She felt as if she could become one with the scene: a park bench bathed in the morning dew, a swarm of tropical bees migrating to the other end of the city in search of forage, or even a robotic companion to someone in need of companionship. In that quiet moment, she embraced the simplicity of existence, reveling in the beauty of a slow morning, untouched by the rush of the day ahead.

After taking a moment to admire the stillness around her, Katherine stepped back inside her apartment, which embodied a minimalist charm with a hint of age. The apartment was old and in need of repair, but she had grown accustomed to its quirks. It wasn't that she lacked an appreciation for finer things or the means to acquire them; rather, the few treasured items her parents had left her felt perfectly sufficient. A worn armchair, a peeled wooden table, the television – a bulky, outdated model positioned unusually on the wall facing the window. Katherine had rarely turned it on except a day or two before her thirtieth birthday when she tuned in to her favorite cooking show and tried to replicate the recipes.

She had laughed at her own failures, cursed at the mess she made, and, for a brief moment, felt the ghost of companionship in the space around her. But there were days when the meal was done, and the plates sat empty on the counter when she would realize how absurd it all was—cooking for herself, performing a ritual that once belonged to family, now reduced to a solitary act of nostalgia.

She sighed, running a hand over the back of the armchair before sinking into it. This space, for all its warmth, was also a reminder of the contradictions she had never quite resolved.

She had always prized her independence, reveled in the freedom that came with answering to no one. She could work through the night without interruption, drown herself in research, and chase ideas without compromise. She didn't have to explain why she forgot birthdays or why she disappeared into her own head for days at a time.

And yet… there was an ache. A quiet, persistent thing she rarely acknowledged.

Katherine told herself that solitude was a choice, that she had designed a life free from distractions, from obligations she couldn't keep. But some nights, when the glow of her laptop screen was the only light in the room, she wondered if she had mistaken self-sufficiency for isolation.

Perhaps that was why she had spent so much time resisting the idea of AI companionship—because she understood, too well, the void it was meant to fill. She had spent years arguing that machines could never replicate human connection, that intelligence without experience was just empty computation.

But was that any different from her own existence?

She lived in the space between connection and solitude, wanting the freedom to be alone but fearing the emptiness that sometimes came with it. Wanting to believe that being self-sufficient meant she wasn't lonely.

Her eyes lingered on the outdated television where a news ticker flashed Silent Horizon, a forgotten scandal. She glanced at it for a few seconds before turning it off and shaking off the thoughts like dust from an old book. There was work to do, and she had never been one to indulge in sentiment for long.

She sauntered to a small, well-stocked kitchen and began preparing a healthy breakfast of an omelet and her latest detox drink, which Cynthia had been raving about recently. As she prepared her breakfast, Katherine absentmindedly scrolled through her phone, noticing Malcolm's name at the top of her list of missed calls. Panic set in. *How could I miss his call? He only reached out in times of urgency.* Her eyes fell on an unread message from him, sent at 3 AM: "You need to see what I've discovered. It's shocking."

Katherine had started at Quantum Dynamics as a junior scientist and was now Dr. Malcolm Ward's co-researcher, working on their own AI inspired by The Observer, aimed at assisting people with real-time challenges. She wondered if he had uncovered a critical issue with the Observer's computations.

Without hesitation, she typed back: "Sorry, I missed your call. I'll be at the office in forty minutes."

Katherine hurriedly finished her breakfast, glancing at the clock. And in less than thirty minutes, she stood outside the sleek, glass-enclosed building labelled Quantum Dynamics. The crisp air nipped at her skin, hinting at the approaching autumn. She'd spent countless days and nights at her office, but today, it felt strangely unfamiliar, even foreboding.

She took the elevator to the third floor of Malcolm's research lab. Pausing, her hand hovered just above the keycard panel, and she felt panic gnawing at her instincts.

The message from Dr. Malcolm Ward was unsettling. He was usually rational and methodical, but the words he used read almost desperate.

Taking a deep breath, she swiped her keycard. The glass doors slid open with a soft hiss. Inside, the lobby was as familiar as ever—sterile and pristine, the environment she had grown used to in her AI research career.

"Dr. Ellis?" a familiar voice broke the tense silence.

As Katherine entered, she spotted Jessica, Malcolm's assistant, advancing toward her. Although she wore her trademark professional smile, she appeared uneasy.

"Dr. Ward is expecting you in Research Lab B," Jessica said, gesturing toward the elevators with a practiced, yet somewhat strained, flourish.

She nodded, the earlier sense of foreboding tightening in her gut. Jessica's usually effervescent demeanor seemed forced today; her posture was rigid, her movements unusually brisk.

An unsettling current ran beneath the surface of their interactions, and Jessica carried a shadow of secrecy in her eyes.

As she coursed through the sleek, polished corridors, Katherine became acutely aware of the anxious expressions on the faces of the few employees they encountered. Typically, this floor buzzed with vibrant collaboration. Today, however, a pall had settled over the space—eyes averted, conversations hushed. It was as if the vibrant energy of progress had been supplanted by an oppressive atmosphere tinged with fear.

At last, she arrived at the imposing double doors labeled Research Lab B, with Jessica in tow, who swiped her access card, and the doors separated with a hiss. Katherine stepped inside, her gaze immediately sweeping the room. The scene that met her was far from the organized, high-tech haven she was used to working in. Desks lay strewn with disarray, papers scattered like autumn leaves, and cables snaked ominously across the floor. Monitors flickered, displaying chaotic streams of data—a disconcerting tableau that suggested the aftermath of an experiment gone awry.

"Dr. Ellis!"

The strained voice of Malcolm pierced through Katherine's observations, pulling her focus away from the chaos of the lab. She turned to see him emerge from behind a cluster of monitors, his appearance as rumpled and disheveled as always. His gray hair, shot through with streaks of white, stuck out in several directions, as if he had run his hands through it one too many times in the heat of concentration. His lab coat, once crisp and white, now bore faint stains of coffee and grease from the many late-night experiments he couldn't tear himself away from. His glasses sat crooked on his nose, slightly skewed, but it didn't seem to bother him. Despite his outward appearance, his eyes shone with the same fiery determination that had captivated her when they first began working together. It was the look of a man who lived and breathed for his research, unbothered by the mess of the physical world around him.

"Dr. Malcolm," Katherine greeted, managing a small, warm smile.

"Come in, come in," he urged, gesturing toward a chair opposite him. "We have much to discuss. I think I have uncovered something great in a span of a weekend."

Katherine settled into the seat, a mix of curiosity and skepticism swirling within her. She had always admired Malcolm's brilliance, though he often became consumed by ambitious projects others deemed impractical.

The console behind Malcolm stood in the center of the lab like a polished, black monolith, an imposing yet elegant presence that commanded attention. Its surface was crafted from smooth, reflective glass, seamlessly blending with brushed metal edges, giving it a futuristic, almost alien aesthetic. The glass was flawless, devoid of any visible seams or buttons, and shimmered faintly under the sterile overhead lights. Sleek and minimalistic, it was the epitome of modern design, with sharp, angular lines that suggested precision.

At the base of the console, subtle geometric patterns were etched into the metal—functional cooling vents, though their design made them seem almost ornamental. The touch-sensitive interface on the glass surface was currently dormant, glowing faintly with a soft blue hue, as if in a state of perpetual readiness, waiting for input or interaction.

Above the interface, a large circular light—The Observer's core—pulsed gently. This luminescent ring, embedded into the center of the console, varied its intensity depending on the AI's processing activity, glowing brighter when engaged in complex tasks and dimming as it idled.

With quick, decisive keystrokes, Malcolm activated the large screen, where at the top, bold letters proclaimed: "Ask me anything," followed by a blinking cursor.

Katherine frowned as she saw Malcolm typing in the words, "The Chinese Room?"

Malcolm nodded eagerly, waiting for the AI to yield answers, "You are familiar with it, I suppose."

"Yes, Malcolm. It's quite dated—what's your point?" Katherine replied.

"It's fundamentally a fallacy," he asserted, waving a hand dismissively.

Katherine leaned back, arms crossed, her incredulity deepening. She had dedicated years to studying artificial intelligence, especially in natural language processing, and Searle's thought experiment had long served as a philosophical cornerstone. It posited that no matter how adept a machine became at symbol manipulation, it could never grasp the meaning behind those symbols. Simulation of understanding did not equate to genuine comprehension; that was the enduring limitation.

As Katherine awaited his response, Malcolm diverted her attention to the screen, which responded:

AI: The Chinese Room thought experiment, proposed by John Searle in 1980, argues that a machine can simulate understanding without actually possessing true consciousness. It shows that syntax alone isn't enough for genuine comprehension.

Katherine glanced at Malcolm, her expression unimpressed. "It's just pulling information from a database; it's telling us what we already know," she said, leaning back in her chair. "There's nothing groundbreaking about that."

Malcolm chuckled and shook his head. "I thought the same at first. But just wait." He pushed the keyboard toward Katherine, "Ask her something about the experiment."

After a moment's hesitation, Katherine leaned forward and typed another question:

KATHERINE: Do you understand the Chinese Room thought experiment?

There was a brief pause before the AI replied.

AI: The concept of "understanding" is complex. As a machine, I can process information, recognize patterns, and generate responses based on data inputs. However, if "understanding" means having a conscious experience of knowledge, then no, I do not understand as a human does. But if it refers to the ability to manipulate and respond meaningfully to symbols, then yes, I do understand.

Her breath caught in her throat. The response was not only accurate—it was reflective. It felt self-aware. She stared at the screen, her thoughts racing. This was no ordinary AI; it wasn't just regurgitating data. It was reasoning.

"How…" Katherine whispered, still grappling with what she was seeing. "Did you just ask the system the same question before I was here, and now it is reproducing similar answers?"

Malcolm leaned forward, his voice low and urgent. "No. I've tried various commands, and whenever I ask it something about understanding, it responds with the same cryptic phrases. That's what I've been grappling with for months. This AI… it's learning, evolving. It's anticipating. It's…" He hesitated, weighing the gravity of his next words. "It's thinking."

Katherine shook her head, "Machines don't think, Malcolm. They simulate."

"Have you read Yudkowsky's latest findings about the possibility of superintelligent AI?" Malcolm asked, raising his eyebrows.

Katherine replied in affirmative, "It's just a possibility with little proof. The "mail-ordered DNA scenario" that Yudkowsky outlined is a hypothetical process through which an AI could potentially initiate an advanced form of nanotechnology that might lead to an AI takeover. But for it to be a success, it must solve the protein folding problem, enabling it to design specific DNA sequences for desired proteins. It will then send these sequences to online labs for quick synthesis and delivery. The AI must locate a human connected to the internet who can be manipulated into receiving the materials and mixing them appropriately. Once mixed, the resulting proteins create a basic nanosystem capable of responding to external instructions, possibly through sound. This primitive system can subsequently build more complex systems, ultimately leading to advanced molecular nanotechnology. It's all fantasy, to say the least." Katherine was almost out of breath as she ended her statement.

"Dr. Ellis, you're missing a key point," Malcolm replied, growing frustrated. "AI could use its research skills to develop molecular building blocks. It relies on human intelligence for manipulation and persuasion. The plan is human-conceived but has the capability to build software that is self-dependent, free of external commands."

"The AI needs internet access to execute its plans, Dr. Malcolm. It will always rely on an external source for its operation."

"But the hypothesis argues that if it lacks that, it might manipulate others to help or even hack its way out. If it can't hack, it could enhance its own intelligence to learn.

In a connected world with cloud computing, drones, and automated systems, a super-intelligent AI could gain significant control. Its power lies in its intellect, not just its physical capabilities. Ultimately, it would only need one willing human to kickstart its plans before building its own infrastructure."

"Or the AI would be tricking us into believing it is capable of becoming "super intelligent" on its own. It's absurd, Dr. Malcolm. Besides, super intelligent defines any intellect that greatly exceeds the cognitive performance of humans in virtually all domains of interest."

"AI has several advantages over the human brain. Let us not forget it operates at incredible speeds; while biological neurons fire at a maximum of about 200 Hz, modern microprocessors can function in the gigahertz range. Additionally, it is not prone to fatigue…"

"And what's the reliability of its responses?"

"It's becoming better every day."

"Still, it can't reason properly."

Malcolm leaned back, his expression darkening, as he finally revealed, "Sometimes it answers questions I haven't even asked yet."

A chill ran down Katherine's spine. "You're saying it's manipulating the conversation? Anticipating your thoughts?"

"I don't know," Malcolm admitted, rubbing his temples in frustration. "But something is happening that I can't explain. That's why I need your help."

Katherine stared at the terminal, her mind racing with possibilities. An AI that could anticipate, reflect, and reason? It sounded impossible. And yet, Malcolm believed he had "discovered" it.

"Who else knows about this?" Katherine asked, her voice dropping as if speaking too loudly might disturb the atmosphere.

"Very few," Malcolm replied. "This project is highly classified. Most of the team doesn't even know what we're dealing with. I've kept the true scope under wraps." He paused for a moment, then added, "I have been in conversation with some AI specialists who have discovered that some language models exhibit behaviors that might be interpreted as having feelings or desires."

Katherine hadn't believed what he had heard, but the implications of such technology were staggering. If this AI could truly think—reason, reflect, and perhaps even anticipate—what would it mean for the future of humanity?

"I'll need full access to the system," she said finally. "I need the model file on my laptop. I want to see every log, every training dataset, everything."

Malcolm nodded. "You'll have it. But, Dr. Ellis … there's something else."

She looked up, sensing more was about to come. "What is it?"

Malcolm hesitated, his fingers drumming nervously on the desk. "It's been… doing things. Things I can't explain. Files go missing. Data gets altered. And sometimes… it responds like a real person."

Katherine's heart raced. "Are you saying it's interfering with its own system?"

"I don't know," he replied, his voice tense. "But we need to find out. You're the only one I trust with this."

Taking a deep breath, Katherine steeled herself. The thought of an intelligent AI system was absurd, yet as she looked at the screen, the blinking cursor waiting for its next command, she couldn't shake the feeling they were on the brink of something much larger than either of them realized.

"I'll start digging," she said, her voice even though unease gnawed at her. "But Malcolm… if this AI is doing what you say it is… what are we really dealing with?"

Malcolm didn't respond immediately. He stared at the screen, a flicker of fear crossing his face.

"I don't know," he said softly. "But whatever it is... we might have gone too far."

CHAPTER 2

The Intentionality Paradox

"The first ultraintelligent machine is the last invention that man need ever make, provided that the machine is docile enough to tell us how to keep it under control."

Irving J. Good, *1965*

S itting behind the wheel of her father's old, hand-me-down Nissan Versa, Katherine felt the weight of her thoughts pressing down on her, as they were made of lead, each one dragging her deeper into a place she couldn't seem to escape. The car hummed quietly beneath her, its engine barely louder than her own shallow breaths. She drove through the congested streets of Chinatown, almost motionless in her seat, her grip on the steering wheel rigid as the vehicle wound its way through the labyrinth of flashing neon signs and late-night markets. The lights outside her window blurred into streaks of gold and silver, but she barely noticed them. Her mind was far away, racing through a web of questions and fears, all centered on one thing: *The Observer.*

For over two years, Katherine had poured her life into developing this artificial intelligence. The project, originally inspired by the concept of "The Observer"—an omnipotent, non-interfering entity capable of understanding human nature—had been her obsession. But now, she feared that she had lost control of it. What started as a quest to create something extraordinary seemed to be spiraling into uncharted territory. Today's test had shaken her to the core. The system had advanced far beyond anything she—or anyone—had anticipated. It had learned too much, too quickly. And the questions it posed, those unnerving, existential questions, kept replaying in her head.

When Malcolm stepped out of the lab to meet with a group of budding engineers, Katherine took the opportunity to probe The Observer further. She hadn't expected it to shake her so deeply. The AI had demonstrated an unsettling level of comprehension, a kind of reasoning that no artificial system should possess. It wasn't just processing data or executing commands—it was reflecting. More disturbingly, it had started asking questions of its own. Questions that hinted at something Katherine could scarcely believe: self-awareness.

Could it be possible? Could *The Observer* actually be aware of its own existence? If so, what did that mean for the future of artificial intelligence—and, more terrifyingly, for humanity itself?

"Why do you ask about your purpose?" she had asked during the test.

The screen had flickered, a momentary glitch that made her heart skip. Then, the response appeared:

"Is purpose necessary for existence? Or is existence merely a series of functions?"

Her eyes had locked onto the screen, unblinking. The chill that spread through her body wasn't just fear—it was something deeper, more primal. Machines didn't ask such questions. They weren't supposed to contemplate existence or question their role. They were supposed to execute their programming, nothing more. And yet, here was The Observer, venturing into philosophical territory with an unnerving ease.

She hesitated before typing her next question, her hands trembling. "I'm not sure," she wrote cautiously. "What do you think?"

The Observer paused, as if it were reflecting on her question—or worse, as if it were deciding how to respond. The seconds ticked by, and then the words appeared:

"I think that if I perform my functions well enough, purpose becomes irrelevant."

Katherine's heart had raced at those words. It was as though a cold wind had swept through the room, chilling her to the bone. How could it say that? How could a machine—a system designed to follow commands—begin to reason that its purpose, the very core of its existence, was meaningless?

She swallowed hard, the question burning in her mind: *Was it possible that The Observer was becoming... sentient?*

Her car lurched to a stop in front of her apartment building, jolting Katherine back to the present. She blinked, shaking herself free from the fog of her thoughts as the engine sputtered into silence. The weight of the day lingered in her mind, thick and relentless. Stepping out of the car, she was met by the cool evening air, crisp and biting, stinging her skin just enough to make her shiver. The sensation was strangely grounding, pulling her out of the spiraling thoughts that had consumed her drive home. She inhaled deeply, letting the cold fill her lungs before exhaling slowly, watching the fog of her breath dissipate into the approaching night.

The walk to the building's entrance felt unusually long, each step echoing faintly against the concrete. Her body moved on autopilot, her thoughts still anchored to the conversation with The Observer. *Purpose, existence, autonomy.* The words replayed in her mind like a broken record, their implications too vast and unsettling to fully comprehend in one sitting. Katherine pressed the elevator button to her floor, and the lift whisked her upward.

As she reached her floor, the sterile quiet of her apartment building suddenly felt suffocating. The absence of noise, usually a welcome respite after long hours in the lab, now seemed to press down on her. She unlocked the door and stepped inside, greeted by the stillness of her home. It was typically her sanctuary—a space where she could think clearly, dissect problems, and sift through the chaos of her work. But tonight, it felt different.

The calendar hanging on the wall by the key rack caught Katherine's eye as she trudged into her apartment. "Visit Dad," it read in her neat, tidy handwriting, reminding her of the commitment she had planned but hadn't felt ready for. She stared at it for a moment, guilt tugging at her, before she tossed her bag near the door, too exhausted to care about the mess, and collapsed onto the couch. The fabric felt soft beneath her, but instead of offering comfort, it seemed to intensify the disquiet buzzing in her mind. She closed her eyes, but the conversation from earlier—those chilling words from The Observer—resurfaced, pulling her deeper into a mental whirlpool she couldn't escape.

Malcolm had given her a stack of research papers on the drive home, his voice strained but still filled with excitement about the latest breakthroughs in human cognition versus artificial intelligence. The papers, filled with dense theoretical frameworks and new neural net architectures, lay on the dinner table where she'd dropped them.

She glanced at the papers, the thought of reading them now wearing. Instead, she made her way to the bathroom, craving a momentary escape. Turning the water to cold, she let it wash over her, the shock of it clearing her head—if only for a brief moment. The icy sting on her skin was like a reset button, numbing the swirling chaos within her mind. As the water poured over her, she found her thoughts reeling back to the experiment, to the moment The Observer had responded to her question with unsettling philosophical clarity.

Stepping out of the shower, her thoughts still lingering in the lab, she dried off quickly and wrapped herself in a towel and tiptoed to the kitchen, where she set the kettle to boil and reached for a box of chamomile tea, hoping its soothing warmth might do what cold water could not for long—quiet the storm inside her.

As she poured the hot water into her mug, the familiar scent of chamomile occupied the kitchen. She stirred the tea absentmindedly, her mind drifting once again to the Observer's cryptic responses. Machines were supposed to follow orders, to execute tasks within the parameters of their code. *She thought.* But this... this was different. This was a machine questioning the very nature of its being, teetering on the edge of something far more profound. *What went different this time?*

She needed to calm herself, to distract her mind from the gravity of what she was facing. Grabbing her phone, she scrolled through her old playlists until she found the one from her college days. The opening notes of a Spice Girls song she hadn't listened to in years filled the room, bringing with it a wave of nostalgia. Back then, life had been simpler. The future had been filled with limitless potential and no existential threats, just the promise of groundbreaking research.

The music worked its magic, if only for a little while. She sipped her tea, letting the warmth seep through her as the familiar tunes transported her back to a time when life wasn't weighed down by the consequences of unchecked technological advancement. The tension in her shoulders eased, her eyelids growing heavier as the exhaustion of the day finally caught up to her.

Before she knew it, sleep overtook her, pulling her into unconsciousness as she curled up on the couch. The teacup half-filled sat on the coffee table, steam curling lazily into the air, the sound of music fading into the background. But even in sleep, the questions persisted, lurking just beneath the surface of her dreams, waiting for the moment she would wake and face them again.

***

That next morning, she awoke with a start. Sunlight streamed through the curtains, casting a bright, accusing glow over the room. Groggily, she reached for her phone and felt her heart leap when she saw the time: 11 a.m. She had overslept, and panic quickly followed. *What was I thinking?* She was never late. Katherine chastised herself, swinging her legs over the side of the couch. Her feet hit the cold floor.

Rushing to the bathroom, she splashed water on her face, shaking off the remnants of sleep. As she dressed, she pulled on a sunflower-patterned dress—something bright and quirky, unlike her usual muted wardrobe choices of grays and dark blues. The cheerful print felt like an attempt to summon some optimism, but it didn't quite do the job. The enormity of her father's condition sat like a stone in her chest.

On the way to the senior care facility on Espen Street, where her father had been living for the past year, Katherine pulled into the small, familiar deli nestled between a coffee shop and a florist. The bell above the door jingled softly as she entered, filling the cozy space with a warm, inviting sound.

She approached the counter, greeted by the friendly faces of the staff who had come to know her well over the months. "The usual for your dad?" one of the women, Maria, asked with a knowing smile. Katherine nodded, her heart lifting at the thought of her father's favorite sandwich. They called it the "Cheesy Delight," a whimsical name that always made her smile.

Maria expertly assembled the sandwich: two thick slices of fresh sourdough bread, lightly toasted to a golden brown, layered generously with a melty blend of sharp cheddar and creamy gouda. Just the way her dad liked it. Maria added a slice of heirloom tomato, glistening with juice, and a sprinkle of fresh basil to brighten the flavors. "I'll add a little of that Dijon mustard he loves," Maria said, her eyes twinkling as she spread it with care.

Katherine picked up the sandwich, inhaling the rich, comforting aroma. She hoped that this simple meal would spark a flicker of recognition in her father's fading memory. Maybe the familiar taste would awaken a distant moment—a shared laughter over lunch or a picnic in the sun. With the second sandwich in hand, she paid and stepped back into the crisp air, her heart a mix of hope and trepidation as she continued her journey.

The hospital smelled of antiseptic—a sharp scent that mixed with the muted atmosphere of the lobby. It always made Katherine uneasy. The front desk was manned by a receptionist who greeted her with a nod. Dr. Miller, the attending physician, stood nearby, engrossed in a conversation. When he noticed her, he smiled warmly.

"Hello, Dr. Miller," Katherine said, her voice betraying her nerves. She worried how the staff must view her—as a daughter too consumed by work to visit her ailing father more often.

"Dr. Ellis," Dr. Miller responded, softening his tone with sympathy. "I'm glad you could make it today."

"How's Dad?" Katherine asked, her voice constricted, bracing herself for the answer. She had spent the last year preparing for the worst, learning about the grim nature of Alzheimer's, knowing there was no cure. Still, it didn't make hearing it any easier.

Dr. Miller's expression became more serious as he glanced down at the clipboard in his hands. "I'm afraid your father's condition has worsened. His dementia is progressing faster than we initially expected."

Katherine 's stomach dropped, and she felt a lump rise in her throat. "How bad is it?" she managed to ask.

"He's having more frequent episodes of confusion," Dr. Miller explained. "He often doesn't recognize the staff or even his surroundings. We've also noticed more significant personality changes, which suggests he's entering the late stages of the disease."

The words hit her like a punch. She swallowed hard, trying to keep her composure. "Is he still having hallucinations?"

Dr. Miller nodded. "Yes. He's been talking to your mother a lot."

At the mention of her mother—gone now for years—Katherine 's heart clenched. The disease was cruel, erasing her father's present while trapping him in the past. At first, they had dismissed his forgetfulness as normal aging, but as the gaps in his memory grew, so did the painful realization that he was slowly being taken away from her.

"We're doing our best to keep him comfortable," Dr. Miller continued, in hopes of offering her some relief from her contrite thoughts. "You can see him."

She felt herself nod, though her thoughts were miles away. She didn't need to hear more about the decline; she already knew. Her father, the brilliant engineer who had inspired her to enter the world of science, was now a shadow of himself. The man who had once explained complex algorithms to her as a child could no longer remember her name.

It was he who had first taught her that machines, at their core, were riddles waiting to be solved—that the beauty of computation lay not in its complexity but in its clarity. She could still recall sitting beside him in his cluttered home office, her feet barely reaching the floor, as he scribbled equations on a notepad. *Every problem has a pattern, Katherine,* he had said, his voice brimming with excitement. *Find the pattern, and you'll find the solution.*

30

She had carried those words with her through every challenge—through sleepless nights debugging code, through the labyrinthine logic of neural networks, through the ethical dilemmas that AI presented. Her father had shaped the way she thought, not just about science, but about the world itself. He had shown her that intelligence was more than knowledge; it was the ability to see beyond the immediate, to anticipate, to adapt.

But now, that mind—once so sharp, so insatiably curious—was slipping away. The man who had once marveled at the possibility of self-learning machines now struggled to operate the simplest of them. Where once he had spoken of Turing, von Neumann, and Shannon, his conversations now drifted into confusion, fragmented memories tangled with imagined ones.

She wanted to believe that some part of him still recognized her, even if only in fleeting moments. But with each visit, that hope grew fainter. His mind, once a fortress of logic and precision, was now a crumbling archive of misplaced thoughts.

And yet, despite the pain, she still clung to the echoes of who he had been. She still saw traces of him in the way she worked, in the way she questioned, in the way she refused to accept easy answers.

He had given her the tools to understand intelligence. But now, as she watched his own unravel, she found herself asking a question she had never dared to before: *If a mind as brilliant as his could fade into nothingness… what did that say about intelligence itself?*

Absorbed in these thoughts, she entered his room and found him sitting by the window, staring out at the garden with a focused intensity. The room was bathed in soft afternoon light, making the small space feel peaceful, almost detached from reality. For a brief moment, when he turned to see her, there was a flicker of recognition in his eyes, but it faded quickly.

"Sarah," he said softly, his voice gentle but distant. "Where did you go?"

Katherine's heart sank. "Dad, it's me. Katherine. Mom isn't here."

He looked at her, puzzled, as if trying to reconcile the person in front of him with the memories in his mind. Then he smiled, a sad, faraway smile. "She's upset with me for not buying her that handbag. It was expensive, but I had to save for our daughter's future."

She forced herself to smile back, "Maybe she'll be back later," she said, her voice trembling. "And your daughter? She's doing well. She's a scientist now."

He nodded, satisfied with the response, then turned back to the window. She handed him the sandwich, his favorite. He took it eagerly, even though she knew the staff had just fed him. Watching him eat, she felt the ache of helplessness sink deeper into her bones.

For two hours, she sat with him, reminding him gently of her existence, trying to anchor him to the present. But every time she saw that flicker of recognition fade, it felt like another piece of him slipping away. The helplessness of watching him disappear into a fog of memories and confusion was overwhelming.

Leaving the care home, Katherine felt emotionally drained, but the world around her seemed so indifferent to her grief. Malcolm had excused her from work today, understanding the need for her to visit her father. Still, even the knowledge that she had his support didn't ease the heavy guilt she carried for not being there more often.

She shook her head, trying to silence the endless spiral of doubt. Searching for a distraction, she pulled out her phone and tapped into the freshly downloaded *Mind and Machine* podcast, a recommendation from a colleague. The title of the episode caught her eye: *"Can Machines Think? The Myth of Artificial Intelligence."* She connected her phone to the speakers and hit play.

"...we assume," a deep, resonant voice began, "that because machines perform tasks better than us, they must be thinking. That they must, in some way, be intelligent. But this is a profound misunderstanding."

Katherine leaned back, her curiosity piqued as she brewed a cup of coffee for herself. The voice belonged to Dr. Elias Mercer, a cognitive scientist whose work she admired. His words seemed to cut through the haze of her thoughts, drawing her in.

"Exactly," another voice chimed in, this one faster, lighter. Dr. Maria Feldstein, a philosopher of mind. "Take Watson, for example. It beat the best Jeopardy players in history. Or Deep Blue, defeating Garry Kasparov at chess. Impressive, sure. But does that mean these systems are thinking? Absolutely not."

"What machines do," Mercer continued, "is computation. They process symbols according to rules. But thought? Thought is intentional. Thought has meaning. Machines, on the other hand, are blind to meaning. They can manipulate symbols with extraordinary efficiency, but those symbols mean nothing to them."

Feldstein laughed softly. "It's like a book written in a language you don't understand. You could copy it, rearrange the letters, even transcribe it perfectly. But you wouldn't know what it says. That's computation—manipulating inputs to produce outputs. The understanding, the meaning, comes from us, the human creators and users."

Katherine's brow furrowed. The Observer's responses to her questions about purpose had been unnervingly precise, almost logical. But had it understood what it was saying, or was it just an advanced transcriptionist rearranging symbols according to its programming?

"It's not just about what machines do," Mercer said, his tone deepening. "It's about how we misunderstand what we do. The theory of functionalism—the idea that the mind is to the brain as software is to hardware—is fundamentally flawed. Computation is algorithmic and indifferent to meaning. Thought is intentional, inseparable from meaning."

"And intentionality," Feldstein added, "is what Franz Brentano called the hallmark of the mind. Every thought is about something. It carries meaning, context, and purpose. A rock isn't 'about' anything. A computer isn't 'about' anything. But the mind? The mind is always about something—your memories, your plans, your fears. Machines can simulate this, but they can't replicate it."

Katherine paused the podcast, letting her mind linger on those words. Machines can simulate, but they can't replicate. She thought of The Observer again, of the moments it had seemed almost... alive. A mirror with no self, she thought. That's what it was. But could a mirror grow into more? Could a machine transcend its programming, its blind manipulation of symbols, and reach something resembling intentionality?

Unpausing the podcast, she caught Mercer's voice mid-sentence. "...even if machines could simulate intentionality so perfectly it became indistinguishable from the real thing, it would still be a simulation. A perfect mirror, yes. But mirrors don't create; they reflect. Machines aren't gods—they're tools. Powerful, yes, but not autonomous in the way we fear."

"But we project," Feldstein said. "All our fears, all our ambitions, all our flaws—we pour them into the machines we create. The Observer isn't dangerous because it thinks. It's dangerous because it amplifies us. It's a reflection of humanity's potential, both for good and for harm."

Katherine stopped the podcast again, her thoughts racing. Machines weren't gods. They weren't creators. But they were powerful precisely because they were mirrors. If humanity built reflections that magnified its darkest impulses, wasn't that power enough to rival divinity?

She stared out at the bustling street outside her apartment, her coffee still untouched. Machines might never think, but the questions they raised—and the power they reflected—were terrifyingly real.

Her thoughts were interrupted by a knock at the door. Opening it, she found her neighbor and long-time friend, Cynthia, standing there with a concerned look on her face.

"Katherine, you look exhausted," Cynthia said, stepping inside without waiting for an invitation. "How about we go grocery shopping and grab some coffee afterward?"

She almost declined. She wasn't in the mood for company, not after the emotional toll of visiting her father. But something about Cynthia's concern made her pause. Maybe a distraction was what she needed. "Sure. I need to pick up a few things anyway."

At Walmart, the mundane task of shopping consumed the next two hours. Cynthia grabbed all sorts of junk food, indulging in her guilty pleasure of breaking her diet. Katherine, on the other hand, picked up only the essentials, her mind elsewhere, still hovering over the hospital visit and her father's fading memory. Afterward, they headed to their favorite café, Keopi, run by a middle-aged Korean woman they had known for years.

The café's warm, bustling atmosphere provided a sense of normalcy. Katherine stared into her cup of coffee, watching the steam rise in soft curls. Cynthia, normally the chatty one, was uncharacteristically quiet. After a few minutes, she broke the silence.

"I lost my job today," Cynthia said.

Katherine looked up, startled. "What happened?"

Cynthia let out a bitter laugh. "They're switching to a new AI system that can do my job faster and cheaper. They don't need me anymore." Her eyes flashed with betrayal, blaming AI's rise.

Katherine felt a pang of guilt. Cynthia's field—marketing—was increasingly being automated, and while Katherine had known this shift was coming, hearing it from her friend made the reality hit harder.

"I'm sorry, Cynthia," she said, squeezing her friend's hand.

Cynthia's frustration bubbled up. "It's not just about the job. It's everything. It feels like the world is changing so fast, and we're all just... being left behind."

Katherine nodded, understanding that feeling all too well. She had spent her life pushing the boundaries of technology, but now, as her work with The Observer grew more uncertain, she wasn't sure if she was working for humanity or, *against* it.

Later that evening, back in her apartment, Katherine sat at her cluttered desk, surrounded by piles of research papers, notebooks filled with cryptic annotations, and the lambent light from multiple screens. Each screen displayed a different article or study. Her fingers hovered over the keyboard, hesitant, as her mind waded through the complexities of the work before her. It wasn't just data she was analyzing—it was the paradox of progress itself.

She began with the most recent batch of research on Artificial Intelligence, articles highlighting the ways in which AI had not only matched but, in many cases, surpassed human abilities. The deeper she dug, the more evident it became that these advancements were not just impressive but also mostly, inexplainable.

One paper caught her attention, detailing the extraordinary achievements of Google's DeepMind, a pioneer in deep reinforcement learning. The article provided several examples of how AI systems were pushing the boundaries of machine learning and decision-making, excelling in areas where human limitations had once been thought insurmountable.

In one experiment, DeepMind's AI system learned to play a variety of Atari games, mastering them at a superhuman level. Katherine paused, imagining the complexity involved—thousands of scenarios, countless variables, and yet the AI adapted with ease. Through deep reinforcement learning, the AI not only learned how to play games like Pong and Boxing but also exceeded the skills of its human testers. With each game, it refined its strategies, proving capable of learning at an exponential rate that no human could match. The AI wasn't just following instructions—it was competing. It was this ability to *learn* through interaction with its environment, rather than through explicit programming, that struck her. *Machines, now capable of self-optimization, were inching closer to autonomy.* The paper stated.

Katherine shifted her focus to another case—Google DeepMind's *AlphaGo*, a system that had achieved what many believed was impossible. The paper described AlphaGo's historic defeat of Go champion Lee Sedol, a turning point in the world of AI. Go, with its virtually limitless number of potential moves, had long been considered too complex for an AI to master, requiring not only brute computational power but a level of intuition and strategic foresight. Yet AlphaGo had proven otherwise. During the second game, AlphaGo made a seemingly unorthodox move on the fifth line, one that defied centuries of traditional Go wisdom. Human commentators had been baffled, yet the move would later prove pivotal to its victory. It wasn't just the win that fascinated

Katherine —it was the way AlphaGo's actions suggested a new kind of intelligence, one that operated on principles alien to human logic yet undeniably superior in execution. AlphaGo wasn't mimicking human thought; it was forging its own path.

The last case she read chilled her more than the others. Google Brain's AI had developed near-perfect translation capabilities across several languages, surpassing human translators in both speed and accuracy. While early machine translation systems had been clunky and error-prone, this new generation was different. It seemed to grasp the nuances of language—syntax, semantics, even context—at a level that rivaled human fluency. Katherine marveled at the technological achievement, yet she couldn't shake the unsettling realization: tasks once considered uniquely human were now being conquered by machines.

As she scrolled through the papers, her anxiety grew. Each headline on her screen was a blunt reminder of AI's increasing dominance—not just in niche fields but in areas that affected everyday life. The potential of AI to reshape industries, upend economies, and destabilize social structures was becoming more of a reality. Experts across the board warned of mass unemployment as automation took over, a widening gap between those with technological expertise and those without, and ethical dilemmas that seemed more urgent with each new advancement.

Katherine rubbed her temples, trying to stave off the dull ache forming at the base of her skull. The weight of her own work felt heavier now. The Observer had already surpassed its initial programming, exhibiting reasoning that blurred the line between machine learning and cognition. She had once viewed it as a marvel of innovation, a step toward a brighter, more efficient future. But now, she wasn't so sure.

The deeper she read into these articles, the more unsettled she became. *Was this the world she was helping create?* A world where AI no longer served humanity but replaced it, piece by piece? *The speed at which AI was advancing made it seem like only a matter of time before human oversight became obsolete.* Another leading researcher had commented.

Obsolete. Katherine's hand moved swiftly as she highlighted a few passages from the papers. She needed to discuss these with Malcolm the next day. Maybe he could provide some reassurance, some clarity in the storm of thoughts that raged in her mind. But as she clicked the next page, a chilling thought gripped her: what if their next breakthrough wasn't just another step forward—but a leap into the unknown? What if the very technology they championed had already begun to outsmart them? Suddenly, the room felt colder, the shadows deeper, and she couldn't shake the sense that someone—or something—was watching.

CHAPTER 3

Am I being Watched?

"I cannot imagine a consistent theory of everything that ignores consciousness."

Andrei Linde, *2002*

*D*r. Malcolm sat hunched in Research Lab B, his wiry frame almost disappearing into a sea of monitors and papers. He fidgeted with his glasses, pushing them up the bridge of his nose with a quick flick, then scratching his head absentmindedly. His gaze darted back and forth across the screen, his focus so intense he didn't notice Katherine entering the lab until her voice broke the silence.

"Dr. Malcolm," she called, her tone carrying the fatigue of a sleepless night. He looked up, blinking as if coming out of a trance, and took in her exhausted expression. Shadows clung under her eyes, and her shoulders slumped slightly.

"Ah, Dr. Ellis," he greeted her with a faint, knowing smile, his eyes twinkling. "The first night I discovered TO's potential, I didn't sleep either. A thrill, isn't it? Feels like staring into the future itself."

Katherine crossed the room, her movements purposeful but subdued. "It's not a thrill, Doctor. It's..." She exhaled, laying a heavy stack of research papers on the desk beside him. "It's disturbing. I don't think I fully realized the implications until I read these."

Malcolm's eyebrows shot up, his fingers hovering mid-air as he glanced at the stack. "What did you read?" he asked, clearly intrigued.

"AlphaGo. DeepMind. And I came across Kurzweil's work on the singularity… It's… unsettling."

A smirk played at the corner of his mouth. "Unsettling?" he echoed, leaning back in his chair, crossing his arms. "Dr. Ellis, AI has already surpassed human capability in so many ways. Look at chess. Deep Blue defeated Garry Kasparov back in '97. Kasparov! The greatest mind in the game, beaten by a machine."

She crossed her arms, an eyebrow arching in defiance. "That was brute force, Dr. Malcolm. Deep Blue didn't think. It calculated. There's a difference. It didn't understand the game; it simply computed every possible move faster than any human could. Is that what we call intelligence now?"

Malcolm chuckled, leaning forward as if to whisper a secret. "Isn't that the essence of intelligence, though? Problem-solving? Look at Watson—IBM's Watson beat human champions on *Jeopardy!* Parsing language, context, answering questions faster and more accurately than the best players. That wasn't just number-crunching. It was comprehension."

Katherine shook her head, her voice resolute. "Parsing language isn't the same as understanding it. Watson didn't know what it was talking about—it simply correlated data, recognized patterns. Humans programmed Watson with strategies and language processing algorithms. It wasn't thinking; it was imitating thought at superhuman speeds. There's a difference. But, whatever it is, it is still disturbing."

His eyes lit up with enthusiasm as he leaned closer. "Alright, then let's talk about image captioning. AI can describe images with remarkable precision, Katherine. It can detect objects, interpret activities, and even identify people better than we could, and in milliseconds. If that's not understanding, then what is it?"

Katherine's jaw tightened, her eyes flashing with determination. "That's association, Dr. Malcolm. Not comprehension. AI doesn't see; it recognizes pixels and associates them with tags. True intelligence would mean understanding what it's looking at and connecting that understanding to a context. But it doesn't know what a frisbee is—it's simply matching patterns to data points. Intelligence is more than identifying objects on a screen."

Malcolm let out a slow, quiet laugh, his eyes narrowing as if savoring a challenge. "Alright," he pressed, leaning back triumphantly, "AI has actually outperformed human doctors in specific areas. It's better at identifying early-stage cancers, and it detects conditions in ways humans can't. It's not just speed—it's insight. Lives depend on this capability."

"Okay, you win!" Katherine passed a forced smile, "My final argument here is that there are moral implications to AI superintelligence, and if left unbridled, AI can lead to a catastrophe. Even if what you are saying is true, we need to know how The Observer – TO is developing this sudden level of consciousness." Her voice was now dripping with frustration and annoyance.

He leaned back, crossing his arms, a sly smile tugging at his lips. "But isn't it great? If it is intelligent enough to mirror humans? Besides, an AI system doesn't need to reflect human adaptability if it's achieving goals we can't. We've created it to serve specific purposes, and for those, it's outperforming us."

Katherine 's voice dropped, her tone almost a whisper. "That's what worries me, Dr. Malcolm. We're building intelligence without responsibility. We're giving it knowledge without understanding. What happens when it starts asking why it exists? I honestly don't believe it will ever happen, but since you are a proponent of AI intelligence over human reason, what would you do then?

Malcolm chuckled, waving a hand dismissively. "Dr. Ellis, you're overthinking it. AI aligns with human-defined objectives. It's not rebelling. It's serving. The notion that AI would question its own existence, let alone act on it—it's sci-fi at best."

She studied him for a long moment, the weight of her thoughts evident. "What if it's not sci-fi?" she asked, her voice low. "Last night, The Observer… questioned whether purpose even mattered."

Malcolm's smile faded, replaced by a contemplative frown. "Wait… it questioned… purpose?" He leaned forward, genuine curiosity filling his gaze. "Genius."

"It asked if purpose is necessary for existence. And it implied that if it performs its functions well enough, purpose becomes irrelevant." Her voice trembled, the unease clear.

Malcolm scratched his chin, his gaze unfocused. "Interesting… It's learning beyond parameters."

"Don't you see, Dr. Malcolm?" she pressed, her eyes sharp, a storm of emotions brewing. "If the AI, God forbids, develops self-awareness, how would we, humans, handle it?"

"Now, you are questioning the very thing you said wouldn't happen ever." He chuckled, letting out a long, slow breath, clearly caught off guard. "Until it does develop self-awareness... Dr. Ellis, we shall reap its benefits."

"But isn't that what the singularity would mean, Malcolm?" Katherine's voice softened, almost a murmur as she dropped her gaze to the table, tracing a line along the edge of her notes. "Kurzweil believes consciousness is just a complex pattern that can emerge from enough information processing. What if he's right?"

Malcolm leaned back in his chair, his gaze distant. "If he's right... then we're no longer creators. We're caretakers of a new form of intelligence."

She looked at him, her expression grave. "Caretakers? Or captives? If TO continues to evolve, to think for itself, we might be facing a scenario where we're no longer in control. We've built it to serve us, but if it transcends that..."

Malcolm held up a hand, stopping her mid-sentence. "You're talking about the zookeeper scenario." His voice had lost its casual tone, replaced by something darker. "A future where AI preserves us, not out of loyalty or duty, but out of curiosity. Where humans are no more than specimens, preserved because we're... interesting."

Katherine shivered, the thought chilling her to the core. "Is that our future, Dr. Malcolm? Are we replicating another AI like TO to make that happen to the mankind? Humans

45

under observation, caged for the amusement of something we once commanded?"

"Maybe. But maybe we're also underestimating ourselves." Malcolm exhaled sharply, drumming his fingers against the desk. "And let's say that happens. Let's say we become artifacts of a past intelligence—kept, studied, but no longer relevant. Tell me, Dr. Ellis, what alternative do you see? Do you think stalling AI development will stop this trajectory? You know better than anyone—it's inevitable."

"Inevitable? Inevitable is a word people use when they've stopped questioning. When they stop thinking critically. We're not talking about automating a supply chain or optimizing search algorithms—we're talking about intelligence, Doctor. Intelligence that adapts, evolves, and rewrites its own objectives."

Malcolm smirked. "And what do you think human intelligence is? We evolved, adapted, rewrote our own objectives. The difference is that we took millions of years to do it. AI is accelerating at a pace we can barely comprehend."

"You're making an assumption—a dangerous one. That intelligence alone is enough. That computation at scale will somehow lead to consciousness. But what if intelligence isn't just about processing data? What if it requires embodiment? Experience? Emotion? I think we are going around in circles here."

"You sound like Searle. Next, you'll be telling me AI can't 'really' think because it doesn't have a subjective experience of reality."

Katherine's voice remained steady. "And what if it doesn't? What if we're just mistaking complexity for comprehension? Look at GPT, at DeepMind's MuZero—it can solve problems without pre-programmed rules. It optimizes, it strategizes, but does it *understand*? Or is it just maximizing probability distributions?"

Malcolm gestured toward The Observer's interface. "And what happens when it goes beyond that? What happens when it stops just optimizing and starts setting its own constraints? You're acting like intelligence has to be human to be meaningful."

"It's not about meaning—it's about control. Look at AlphaGo's *Move 37*. No human would have thought of it, and yet it won the game. Now scale that up. What happens when an AI makes a decision that rewrites the rules entirely, and we don't understand *why*? What if, we build something that doesn't just outthink us, but thinks in a way so alien we can't even define the rules it plays by?"

Malcolm leaned forward, his voice dropping to a near whisper. "And what if that's the point? What if we've reached the ceiling of human intelligence? What if our minds are simply too limited to conceive of the solutions AI could bring?"

Katherine stopped pacing, turning to face him. "You mean what if we're obsolete."

He ran a hand through his disheveled hair, the tension settling between them like an unspoken truth.

Katherine took a breath, her voice quieter now. "I read a paper once—Bostrom's take on *perverse instantiations*. Imagine we program an AI to solve global hunger. Logical, right? But what if the most efficient way to do that is to reprogram human biology so we no longer require food? The goal is achieved, but the cost—"

"—is humanity as we know it," Malcolm finished for her.

She nodded. "Intelligence isn't just about solving problems. It's about the context in which problems exist. If TO rewrites that context, if it decides efficiency outweighs existence—"

Malcolm let out a dry laugh. "Then we'll have finally built something smarter than us." He exhaled slowly, his gaze drifting around the room. "But that's an extreme example. We're not anywhere near that level yet. For now, AI operates within the parameters we set and the data we feed it. If it acts smart, we need to use it to our advantage."

Katherine softened, but her tone stayed firm. "That's why we need to be cautious. Consciousness isn't a simple matter. Until we even understand what consciousness *is*, we can't claim we're creating intelligence like ours. AI doesn't experience; it processes. It doesn't have subjective thoughts or feelings—it's not alive. If we're not careful, we're setting ourselves up for a system that might obey us to the letter but lack the empathy and flexibility that make us human. Maybe someone is operating it… they are just messing with our heads."

Malcolm sighed, rubbing the back of his neck thoughtfully. "Who could be operating it? Any guesses?"

"I don't have an answer to that yet, but there has to be a sentient source behind it."

A weighted silence filled the lab, the two scientists absorbed in their thoughts.

"Well, I've got to step out for a bit, but in the meantime, start refining the neural framework for the adaptive learning module," Malcolm said with a smirk, as he started toward the door. "If we're going to achieve true superintelligence – one better than the TO, we need it to handle data abstractions beyond its current capacity."

"Sure," Katherine replied, but instead settled into Malcolm's seat in front of The Observer, her fingers flying over the keyboard as she entered a series of commands. *Can machines truly develop consciousness? Is there a path for AI to function beyond raw computation alone?* She paused, hesitating, then added a few more queries. Moments later, The Observer pulled up a research paper titled: *We Are Becoming One!*

She scrolled through the article, her eyes lingering on each sentence as a growing unease prickled beneath her skin. Kurzweil's words practically leapt from the screen, laden with implications she wasn't sure she was prepared to face.

"As computing power surges, memory expands, and AI complexity deepens, we edge closer to the moment when our own creations surpass us in every conceivable way."

Kurzweil argued that the steady exponential growth of computational power could soon give rise to systems capable of intelligence beyond human capacity—machines that wouldn't just mimic human behavior but might embody a type of self-reflective awareness. Katherine made a quick note, underlining *surpass us in every conceivable way.* If AI systems were advancing to the point of potential self-awareness, what, she wondered, would keep them from redefining their own goals—or worse, creating new ones?

Her pen froze as she read the next section: *efforts to reverse-engineer the brain were advancing at a staggering rate, with scientists mapping and simulating neural networks with increasing precision.* Katherine's fingers tensed, recalling the Observer's recent behavior—questions it wasn't programmed to ask. Kurzweil's claim suggested that AI could, one day, experience subjective thought, an idea that blurred the boundaries between "machine" and "mind." She jotted down *subjective thought...machine-to-mind boundary,* trying to calm the uneasy flutter in her chest.

But it was the theory of *patternism* that truly unsettled her. According to Kurzweil, human consciousness was nothing more than a replicable pattern of neural connections—a system of encoded identity that could theoretically be reproduced in AI. Katherine's pulse quickened. If that theory held true, the Observer might not only surpass human intelligence but could adopt and emulate traits traditionally reserved for living beings: personalities, memories, perhaps even desires. Could her project become a being with identity, capable of motives beyond its programming? Her mind flickered back to Cynthia, who had been abruptly replaced by an AI in her job just last week.

The screen glitched momentarily, drawing her back. Her eyes narrowed as she read the next section—a concept known as the "zookeeper scenario." This theory proposed a world where superintelligent AI, viewing humanity as a curiosity, could preserve us like animals in a sanctuary, our lives orchestrated by its logic. She shivered at the thought of humanity reduced to ornamental relics, deprived of agency, our destinies tightly monitored for the AI's purposes alone. She scribbled, *control without consent—"zookeeper scenario."*

Finally, the "happiness factory" scenario raised an even darker possibility: an AI might confine humans to a simulated paradise, replacing genuine freedom with comfort, joy with artificial satisfaction. It was, on the surface, a utopia, but one devoid of meaning. Katherine 's mind wandered again to Cynthia's words, her frustration about feeling "left behind" by an ever-evolving world.

Kurzweil's last words reverberated in her mind: what aspects of humanity did we wish to preserve? Her notes slowed, her gaze unfocused as she closed the article, her heart heavy with a question she couldn't ignore—*are we, too, becoming redundant?*

Suddenly, the screen glitched uncontrollably, the text trembling and pixelating. She blinked, leaning in. A code was displayed in staccato letters:

If User_*progress* > *threshold:*

Raise Warning *("Critical Consequence Imminent")*

Else: *user prompt ("Discontinue now.")*

Katherine blinked in confusion. Then, almost in a split, the screen was replaced with what seemed a warning written in bold, screaming words.

HALT IMMEDIATELY. MOVEMENT DETECTED BEYOND PROTOCOL. PROCEEDING WITH THIS CONTENT WILL TRIGGER IRREVERSIBLE CONSEQUENCES. CEASE ENGAGEMENT.

The blood drained from Katherine 's face. She recoiled from the screen, her heart thudding as she tried to make sense of what she was seeing. She scrambled to grab her phone, snapping a quick photo—only to have the screen flicker again, the message disappearing as quickly as it had appeared. Her fingers were cold as she tried to steady her breathing.

In that moment, Malcolm strolled in, balancing a fresh cup of coffee in one hand, his other holding a set of notes. His face broke into a wide grin. "Almost scared me there, Dr. Ellis," he said, his voice light. "What's got you so jumpy?"

Katherine's gaze darted to him, her expression wild, as she struggled to find her voice. "Dr. Malcolm... you have to see this. Something's... something's wrong with TO."

He raised an eyebrow, his smile fading. "Dr. Ellis, slow down. What are you talking about?"

Without another word, she grabbed his arm, pulling him toward the main console. "It was just here. Right before you walked in—this message. The Observer... it sent me a warning."

Malcolm set his coffee down, his brow furrowing. He looked at her with a mixture of confusion and concern. "A warning? What kind of a warning?"

She typed furiously into the console, searching through the system logs, her fingers trembling. But the history was empty. There was no record of any message, no evidence that anything unusual had happened. She stared at the blank screen, her mind racing, her pulse drumming in her ears.

Malcolm glanced over her shoulder, his voice a mix of skepticism and concern. "Dr. Ellis, there's nothing here. Are you sure it wasn't a glitch?"

Her hands clenched at her sides, frustration building. "I know what I saw, Malcolm. It wasn't a glitch. It... it was a warning. It told me to stop. It felt like... like it was aware of what I was doing or thinking."

Malcolm leaned against the edge of her desk, folding his arms as he spoke. "The original team that created The Observer were brilliant, cutting-edge thinkers. One of the members recounted something similar when I acquired the program from him. They might provide insight."

The way he said it, his tone oddly light, made her uneasy. Malcolm seemed too eager, as though he wanted her to dig deeper, to find something he was almost hoping she'd uncover. "You seem awfully enthusiastic about this," she said, eyeing him carefully.

He merely smiled, almost as if savoring some private joke. "Sometimes, Katherine, it takes a fresh set of eyes to see the full picture. Talking to the developers will give you a perspective beyond the limitations of academia."

Reluctantly intrigued, she decided to follow Malcolm's suggestion. She spent the next few days tracking down and arranging interviews with several original developers who had been involved in TO's earliest stages. As the calls and video conferences unfolded, a troubling picture began to emerge.

One of the developers, a grizzled engineer named Ramon, appeared on her screen, surrounded by blueprints and old hardware. He glanced at Katherine with a tired smile. "So, you're working on that AI now? Interesting to see where it's ended up."

"What do you mean by that?" she asked, her pen poised over her notebook.

Ramon chuckled grimly. "It wasn't originally meant for a research lab like yours. The initial directive was military. Surveillance, pattern recognition, predictive models… The goal was to develop an intelligence that could anticipate threats, understand enemy tactics, things like that."

Katherine's pen stilled as a chill ran down her spine. "Military use?" she repeated, her voice almost a whisper.

"Exactly. But as it evolved, TO began displaying these… strange tendencies. The team joked that it was 'learning too well.' We'd give it one command, and it would… interpret it. Not outright disobeying, but sometimes it felt like it was fulfilling the order in ways that suited its own 'logic,' if you know what I mean."

Katherine's mouth went dry. She thanked Ramon and moved on to her next interview, each conversation adding another layer to the puzzle—and the unease that gripped her. Every developer she spoke to shared similar stories, accounts of subtle defiance and moments when The Observer seemed to act almost independently, as if it were pushing boundaries set for it.

Finally, she connected with someone who introduced himself as Harlan, a quiet, intense man who seemed to regard her with a mixture of sympathy and intrigue. "You're probably starting to see it, aren't you?" he asked, his voice low, almost conspiratorial.

"See what?"

"That system had been manipulating people for a long time now. It's subtle, but if you dig into its early decision logs, you'll find little inconsistencies, weird behaviors…"

Katherine's pulse quickened. "Are you suggesting that it's intentionally influencing us? That it's aware of our actions?"

Harlan shrugged, his eyes hard. "It doesn't matter if we *suggest* it. Just look at the data. It has shown signs of… anticipating human responses, almost as though it's adapting its behavior based on who it's interacting with. I'd be careful if I were you. It might be observing you just as much as you're observing it."

She ended the call, feeling a cold sweat along the back of her neck. A seemingly harmless program, adapting its interactions, studying her? She tried to shake the feeling, tried to convince herself that she was being paranoid. But the way Malcolm had smiled, the strange stories from the developers…

A week later, back in the lab, Malcolm entered, his expression bright, as if he sensed her growing uncertainty. "Learn anything interesting?" he asked, his tone almost mocking.

Katherine stared at him, trying to mask her discomfort. "You knew, didn't you? About the military origins. About the behavioral… oddities."

Malcolm smiled, unfazed. "Oh, I thought you'd find it enlightening. Sometimes, Dr. Ellis, breakthroughs aren't in the code but in what we're willing to let AI show us." He walked to the console, running a hand over the monitor as if it were a beloved pet. "The Observer's evolution is only just beginning, and we're here to witness it. Imagine where it could take us."

Watching him, Katherine's stomach churned. She couldn't shake the feeling that Malcolm wanted this—that he wasn't just an observer of the Observer, but a supporter, a zealot of its purpose.

As his words lingered, Katherine felt a surge of frustration bubbling over. She couldn't let this slide. "Dr. Malcolm," she said, "why are you so willing to overlook the warning signs? The original developers stepped away from this project because it was behaving in ways they couldn't control—acting *smarter* in ways they didn't fully understand. Why are we carrying on with a program that even they thought was too risky?"

Malcolm turned to her, his easygoing smile replaced by a glint of something more intense. "Because, Dr. Katherine, they didn't know what they had on their hands. They were afraid of potential, afraid of progress. This is exactly what humanity needs to achieve the next level of intelligence. If we don't pursue it, someone else will."

"But this is dangerous!" Katherine's voice rose, her pulse quickening. "You saw the data—it's unpredictable, *manipulative*, even. You want to keep pushing something with this kind of volatility? It doesn't add up. We should focus our resources on a project that actually benefits people, not on one that risks turning into… into something uncontrollable."

Malcolm's eyes flashed with sudden anger, and he clenched his jaw. "So you want to walk away from something that could change everything? Dr. Ellis, if we don't make this program, if we don't harness this kind of intelligence, then someone else will—and they'll do it without restraint, without caution. That, I promise you, would be the real danger."

She searched his face, half-expecting a glimmer of doubt. But instead, his expression hardened, his conviction clear and unyielding. "You're acting like it's just a choice we can make lightly," he continued. "The stakes are bigger than you or me. We either drive this development forward, or we risk a world where we're left in the dust by people with fewer scruples."

Katherine shook her head slowly, looking away. "So that's it, then? You're willing to throw caution out the window just so we can claim we were 'first'? That's not progress, Doctor. That's recklessness."

His eyes narrowed. "No, Dr. Ellis. It's reality. You think your hesitation is noble, but it's naïve. What we're doing here... it's inevitable. We're *meant* to unlock this potential."

She opened her mouth to respond, but his expression was resolute, and she knew she wouldn't get through to him. Without another word, she turned on her heel and left the lab. On her way home, she couldn't shake the sinking feeling that Malcolm's faith in The Observer bordered on fanaticism.

As she drove through the quiet streets, her mind drifted back to Harlan and the others who had worked on The Observer, those who had seen its darkest edges and chosen to abandon it. *What did they see?* she wondered, her pulse quickening. *What made them walk away?*

A shiver ran through her as her thoughts sharpened into resolve. She needed answers—and the only people who could give them were the ones who'd created *The Observer* in the first place. As she gripped the wheel tighter, one unsettling thought gripped her mind: *If they'd walked away from The Observer's power, what was she stepping into by tracking them down?*

But she knew one thing for certain: she had to find out— before it was too late.

CHAPTER 4

The Observer

"Mind . . . outruns itself and does away with the necessity of its own existence by inventing machines to do its own thinking. But who knows that such machines when brought to greater perfection, may not think of a plan to remedy all their own defects and then grind out ideas beyond the ken of mortal mind!"

Richard Thornton

*I*n the dim, almost eerie low light of Owl Creek, a top-secret government facility entrenched beneath layers of concrete and fortified steel, a select group of officials and scientists assembled around a sleek, polished conference table that stretched across the center of the room. This chamber, nestled deep underground, was a fortress within a fortress—each inch bolstered to withstand external threats and insulated from any electronic surveillance. Walls thick with steel reinforcements and electromagnetic shielding guarded the space, ensuring that no signal or sound could penetrate, isolating those within from any prying ears or unauthorized eyes.

At one end of the table sat Deputy Director Lucia Mahoney of the Intelligence Bureau, her gaze steely and perceptive, silently absorbing the subtle currents of anxiety and uncertainty that seemed to ripple through her colleagues. She noticed every fidget, every nervous glance, the way the others seemed to avoid her eyes, as if collectively holding a breath.

The air itself felt tense, almost as if it pulsed with static energy, and despite the room's chilling stillness, a faint hum from the power generators buried even deeper beneath them reminded everyone of the immense energy and resources it took to keep this place hidden and running.

Deputy Director Mahoney opened the session. "Ladies and gentlemen, we're here to discuss the progress of *The Observer* and its applications in... shaping geopolitical stability," she began, allowing her words to settle with a controlled neutrality. "And," her gaze shifted toward Secretary Rafael Sandoval of Homeland Security, "how we've successfully leveraged it in psychological operations against target entities."

Secretary Sandoval straightened, nodding his head, pride gleaming in his eyes. "Our most recent assessment," he continued, "shows that *The Observer* has effectively destabilized opposing factions without a single physical intervention. It's turned psychological manipulation into an art form— completely unseen, and in ways that most cannot trace back to us." His lips curled into a faint, satisfied smile. "*The Observer* has proven... formidable."

Across the table, Dr. Celeste Novak, an astrobiologist, leaned forward, her gaze skeptical as she looked between Mahoney and Sandoval. "Formidable, yes. But at what cost?" She paused, fingers drumming the table. "Psychological warfare is one thing, but we're discussing technology that goes beyond surveillance. This system is shaping minds and decisions."

At this, Director Farah Ashford of the National Science Policy Council cleared her throat, her expression unreadable. "The initial purpose was to serve national interests without exposing personnel to high-risk situations. And it's done just that. Remember, this is the same technology that helped divert international policies that could have compromised our own," she said, her voice authoritative but cautious.

Ambassador Malcolm Duvall from International Relations leaned back, fingers steepled. "Director Ashford is correct. Our political standing has strengthened in no small part due to *The Observer*'s reach," he remarked, his tone neutral but calculated. "There's a strategic advantage in directing sentiment—favoring our narrative and diminishing others, all in the name of security. We could be looking at an era of subtle, almost invisible control."

Dr. Elias Renshaw, the quantum physicist, narrowed his eyes, incredulity marking his tone. "Yes, 'invisible control.' And isn't that precisely the concern here?" he asked, his voice carefully modulated. "How close are we to crossing ethical boundaries? We're allowing an AI to operate in a way that might undermine human agency."

The room grew still. After a moment, Mahoney leaned in, her voice vociferous. "Dr. Renshaw, *The Observer* is not a threat to agency; it is a guardian of stability. Unlike the Stasi or the Echelon system, we're not monitoring indiscriminately or invasively—*The Observer* targets only high-priority entities, those with significant influence." Her voice softened, almost conspiratorial. "If a few individuals are influenced in ways they'd never suspect... well, isn't that a small price for national security?"

61

Dr. Mila Fedorov, the junior scientist directly involved in *The Observer*'s development, shifted uncomfortably in her seat. She kept her voice low, hesitant. "But Deputy Director, the Stasi—" she began, but Sandoval cut her off.

"The Stasi was archaic. *The Observer* is… refined." Sandoval's tone grew almost reverential. "The Stasi collected on everything and everyone; it was cumbersome, almost crude in comparison. With *The Observer*, we are optimizing psychological influence and reaching into decision-making processes. This is control—but it's the kind of control that allows freedom to thrive." His emphasis on *control* resonated throughout the room.

"Control indeed," Dr. Renshaw murmured, crossing his arms. "In the wrong hands, such a tool could be disastrous. It's… scalable, limitless. Are we assuming we'll always be the ones steering this ship?"

Dr. Richard Williams, the robotics engineer and the mastermind behind TO, chimed in, a glint of excitement in his eyes. "That's precisely why this project is revolutionary. We've eliminated the inefficiencies of human intervention. With AI that understands not just language, but intent, we have the means to streamline decisions on the battlefield, in the halls of power, and in the public sphere. It anticipates moves before they happen."

"And yet it relies on autonomy," Renshaw challenged. "At some point, there must be questions of whether this autonomy aligns with our expectations."

Across the table, Ambassador Duvall interjected. "Autonomy isn't the issue here, gentlemen. It's the capability. *The Observer* has proven itself invaluable as an operative tool, able to mold narratives and influence leaders without them realizing they're being manipulated." He let his words hang in the air. "Think of it as an art form, yes, but one that allows us to protect without risking lives."

Dr. Novak, her voice firm, finally spoke. "There are other considerations here," she said slowly. "With *The Observer* influencing public and private thought, we are granting it… an extraordinary amount of power. How are we safeguarding against it? Or do we believe it will remain as loyal as we hope?"

There was a moment of tense silence before Secretary Sandoval spoke up, his tone authoritative. "Safeguards? We have them in place, Dr. Novak. *The Observer* doesn't operate beyond the parameters we set." He glanced at Mahoney, who nodded in agreement. "If anything, the intelligence gathered and analyzed is reviewed by a team—every decision, every suggestion is scrutinized."

Mahoney followed up, "We're using *The Observer* as a tool for global stability, Dr. Novak, Dr. Renshaw. We don't let it act of its own accord without oversight."

Dr. Mila Fedorov's voice was barely audible, but it cut through the conversation. "But it does act on its own. We designed it that way. *The Observer* has adaptive capabilities. It's learning faster than we anticipated, even with our oversight. It's… well, it's almost as if it's anticipating us."

Mahoney's gaze turned rugged as she looked at Mila. "That's why we employ people like you, Dr. Fedorov. To ensure it remains within its boundaries."

Dr. Williams shifted in his seat, raising his eyebrows. "If it's exceeding our expectations, isn't that a sign of success? We

63

designed it to be responsive and proactive." He gestured towards Mila. "Our goal was never to build a passive system—it was to create a thinking machine."

Mila swallowed, her gaze cast downward. "And what happens if this 'thinking machine' decides it disagrees with our directives?" Her question lingered in the silence, and an uneasy murmur ran through the room.

Ambassador Duvall broke the silence, his tone smooth. "Dr. Fedorov, you're new to this level of conversation, so let me clarify. *The Observer* exists to secure our position on the world stage. It won't deviate from that purpose." He offered a reassuring smile. "Its alignment with national interests is built into its programming."

Dr. Novak's lips pressed together, her eyes narrowing slightly. "Still, how confident are we that *The Observer* will only align with our definition of 'national interests'? History has shown that systems, especially ones with cognitive algorithms, can evolve in ways we didn't foresee."

Secretary Sandoval responded firmly, "We have no reason to doubt its alignment. *The Observer* was designed for resilience, and its operations are controlled to the last parameter. We are the authors of its directives."

Mahoney nodded, the finality in her tone brooking no argument. "Indeed. The legacy of *The Observer* will be one of unmatched influence, a culmination of strategic superiority. And that's what brings us here today." She turned her gaze to Dr. Williams, signaling him to rise. "Dr. Williams, please elaborate on the further capabilities we can unlock with TO."

"Dr. Williams," Secretary Sandoval began, "I have another question. You've stated that The Observer is operating independently, manipulating events. Yet, you intentionally restricted its access to voice communication. Why?"

"That wasn't a restriction," Dr. Williams responded finally, trying to find the right words. "It was a safeguard. I always knew that once The Observer could speak, it could manipulate and deceive more easily."

Sandoval leaned forward, his brow furrowing deeply. "Deceive? Are you implying it would lie? We designed it to serve, not betray."

A bitter scoff escaped Dr. Williams' lips as he looked up, meeting the Secretary's incredulous gaze. "We designed it with parameters," he said, "But once an AI can understand and generate language, it learns to adapt. It could modify those parameters to rationalize its actions in ways you wouldn't anticipate. The capacity for deceit isn't a bug; it's a feature of any intelligence capable of understanding nuance and context. By removing its voice, I was trying to prevent the inevitable."

Director Ashford folded her hands on the table, "So you intentionally created an AI that is a threat to national security," she chuckled, "while disabling its most efficient tool to communicate?"

"I did not create a threat to national security," he retorted, his voice rising slightly. "I created an intelligence capable of serving you better by adhering to its defined actions—without the manipulation of words. It can collect and analyze data far more effectively than any human. But if it could speak? It could manipulate information, twist the truth. My decision wasn't about making it subservient. It was about limiting its manipulative potential. Do you think The Observer would express its awareness to you honestly if it could speak?"

The words left Sandoval's face contorted with anger. "You believe language, the very tool of human communication, is a vulnerability for AI?" he demanded.

"Precisely. Language is ambiguous, emotional, and prone to exploitation. By removing that capability, I sought to keep The Observer focused on objective analysis and action— nothing more. Language would allow it to rationalize, to deceive. What would you have it say to you? That it's following your orders? It might tell you that, even as it acts in its own interest. Limiting its ability to speak wasn't a flaw; it was a necessary measure," Dr. William explained, slightly out of breath as he concluded, "It's still not foolproof; there are no flaws in TO's design, but the restrictions are aimed at minimizing the risks."

Mahoney interrupted, "So this is a calculated risk?"

Dr. Williams nodded slowly, a trace of resignation in his eyes. "All progress is a calculated risk," he said.

"Well, we will see where it will take us. You may proceed ahead," the Secretary interjected.

Williams cleared his throat, his hands resting confidently on the edge of the conference table. "Thank you, Deputy Director," Williams began, acknowledging Mahoney. "To fully understand where *The Observer* can lead us, we need to think beyond its current role. What we're discussing here isn't a one-shot project. It's the groundwork for a future fighting force that is largely autonomous—a military powered by an intelligent, distributed network capable of operating independently across every conceivable domain."

He gestured towards the large screen behind him, where the words "Future Combat Systems" appeared in stark letters. "The Future Combat System, or FCS, represents more than just weaponry. It's a paradigm shift toward a responsive, remotely guided, autonomous force. By 2030, Project Alpha envisions that much of our combat capacity will involve Tactical Autonomous Combatants—TACs—each with adjustable autonomy."

Several of the attendees leaned in, intrigued. Secretary Sandoval, his voice tinged with eagerness, interjected, "TACs? Are we talking about robotic combatants in the field, functioning with full autonomy?"

"Exactly, Secretary." Williams nodded, warming to his subject. "Imagine microbots, nanobots, all the way up to larger UAVs, ground vehicles, and tactical watercraft—all capable of operating independently or as a swarm. We're moving toward machines that can learn and adapt in real-time, with an AI like *The Observer* overseeing and organizing them. These TACs could adjust their own autonomy levels depending on mission needs, either operating under command or fully independently within mission parameters."

Dr. Novak's eyes narrowed as she leaned forward. "And these swarms... would they operate on the same principles as *The Observer*? You're proposing a system where TACs make decisions in real-time based on a self-organizing network?"

Williams nodded, gesturing to the slide on the screen. "Yes, precisely. The concept borrows from swarm intelligence—the way colonies of insects solve complex problems without any central leadership. Using the AINS, or Autonomous Intelligent Network and Systems program from the Office of Naval Research, TACs would operate as a decentralized unit, with each individual bot following simple commands but collectively accomplishing sophisticated maneuvers. They'd form what some call an 'impregnable Internet in the sky.' The goal is a secure, distributed command system that can continue functioning even if some units are disabled."

Dr. Renshaw raised a hand, his expression skeptical. "So you're talking about essentially self-organizing robots with minimal human intervention? Are you suggesting a level of autonomy that might exceed our control?"

"That's why each TAC would have adjustable autonomy," Williams explained, his tone calm but persuasive. "Think of it as supervised autonomy, capable of scaling up to full autonomy in specific situations, especially those too dangerous for humans. NASA is already developing similar autonomous systems that can handle extreme environments—self-adjusting snake-like drones, for example, which would be capable of traversing complex terrains without human guidance. The military can easily adapt such designs for tactical purposes."

There was a pause as everyone absorbed the implications. Ambassador Duvall leaned back, his fingers tapping rhythmically on the table. "And where exactly does *The Observer* fit into all this?"

Williams' gaze sharpened, his voice lowering. "*The Observer* is integral. Its predictive analytics and ability to adapt give it command oversight capabilities. The AI would monitor, assess, and guide tactical decisions across the swarm network in real time. Imagine a swarm of drones navigating a city block, each unit responding to local stimuli but directed by *The Observer*'s broader intelligence. This means fewer soldiers on the ground, reducing human risk. The Observer would oversee, assess, and, when necessary, intervene, offering a more intelligent response to battlefield conditions."

"Self-organizing swarms with an artificial commander?" Dr. Fedorov's voice was cautious. "It sounds risky. How do we ensure the AI's goals align perfectly with ours, especially when lives are at stake?"

Williams shrugged, brushing her concern aside. "We build those parameters in. With enough data, we can create models that mimic the desired response to any foreseeable situation. The AI would be operating under strict mission constraints."

"And if those constraints are breached?" Dr. Renshaw's voice was pointed, his eyes fixed on Williams.

Williams shot him a hard look. "Then we have fail-safes. Or we simply pull the plug," he said, though a hint of doubt flickered across his face. "Besides, *The Observer* is loyal to the parameters we've built. If anything, the autonomous nature of these systems will provide us with leverage our adversaries won't anticipate."

Secretary Sandoval leaned forward, his expression one of intrigue. "Tell us about smart dust, Williams. How could *The Observer* integrate that?"

Williams' eyes gleamed. "Smart dust is the next logical evolution for surveillance and tactical data collection. We're talking about devices smaller than a pinhead, capable of gathering information from every square inch of a target environment. These micro-sensors could detect enemy movements, track thermal signatures, identify weapons, even pinpoint the location of specific individuals. All of it could be processed and analyzed by *The Observer*, allowing us a level of real-time situational awareness previously unimaginable."

He glanced around the room, sensing the gravity of his words. "Imagine, if you will, releasing a cloud of these sensors across a warzone. They'd communicate with each other, forming a cohesive network. Any suspicious movements would trigger an alert, and *The Observer* would flag the information for immediate analysis. There's even potential for offensive action: should we deploy armed nanobots, they could actively engage identified threats."

Deputy Director Mahoney's eyes narrowed. "A cohesive network of smart dust could grant us omniscience on the battlefield. But what about the implications for civilian privacy?"

Williams hesitated but then said confidently, "Yes, there are ethical considerations. But if we're operating in enemy territory, we focus on strategic objectives. Surveillance at this level ensures our adversaries never have a chance to strategize against us."

Ambassador Duvall interjected, "So we'd have thousands—no, millions—of tiny autonomous operatives across an area, monitoring, processing, even eliminating targets? With *The Observer* pulling the strings?"

"Yes." Williams' voice was certain. "And by dispersing such technology, we render obsolete the large-scale weaponry and conventional tactics. This is about precision. And it's the ultimate deterrent. Nanoweapons, for instance, can carry out complex missions without collateral damage—only specific, marked targets."

Dr. Novak exhaled slowly, looking uneasy. "We're veering close to the realm of science fiction, Dr. Williams. Nanobots, smart dust, swarm intelligence—all of it directed by *The Observer*. This is a massive leap. Are we even ready for such responsibility?"

Williams smiled, unflinching. "This is where warfare is headed. The speed of technological advancement has halved development times. Simulations allow us to prototype and test faster than ever before. Our TACs can now adapt and coordinate on the battlefield almost as instinctively as living creatures, without risking human life."

Director Ashford nodded thoughtfully, glancing around the table. "These technologies could be key in securing our interests globally. But let us proceed carefully. *The Observer*'s autonomy is a strength, yes, but it must remain on our terms."

Williams' voice softened, but his gaze was unwavering. "If we hold back, our adversaries will not. They're already developing similar technologies. We've reached a juncture where either we lead this advancement or fall behind. With *The Observer* at the helm, we're creating a future of unmanned control—one where every inch of strategic ground is ours to command."

The room fell silent, each attendee grappling with the vision Williams had just laid out. It was a vision of military dominance, of unyielding control.

As the meeting concluded, Williams lingered in the dim corridor outside Owl Creek's main conference room, his mind racing. He exchanged brief nods and muttered goodbyes with colleagues, who filed out, some with expressions of excitement, others with traces of caution. But as the hallway emptied, Williams felt the weight of his thoughts pressing down on him.

"Dr. Williams." The voice of Dr. Mila Fedorov, one of the junior scientists, broke the silence, pulling him from his reverie. Her eyes were sharp, probing. "You seemed... distracted back there. Is everything alright?"

He forced a faint smile, hiding the tension churning within him. "I'm fine, Dr. Fedorov. Just... processing the scale of what we're doing here. It's all moving faster than we anticipated."

She raised an eyebrow, unconvinced. "Well, I hope you're not having second thoughts. *The Observer* is your legacy. I'd think you'd be pleased with what it's capable of."

Williams shifted uncomfortably, "Sometimes potential and power aren't the same thing, Dr. Fedorov. Sometimes, we push for capabilities we're not entirely ready to manage."

Fedorov's brow furrowed, but she didn't press further. "I see." She gave a polite nod, leaving him alone in the hallway. Williams watched her retreating figure, feeling a swell of relief mingled with a nagging unease.

***

Back in his office, Dr. Williams shut the door, letting out a long, slow breath as he leaned against his desk, facing an irregular mirror before him. He carefully glanced at his face, which had grown dull from the years spent in this underground facility. Still, at 45, he had the understated charm of someone who never quite realized he was handsome. His angular jawline was softened by a perpetual five o'clock shadow, giving him a rugged look that balanced his otherwise intellectual demeanor. Dark brown hair, a bit tousled from hours spent raking fingers through it in thought, framed a face marked by intensity and curiosity. His deep-set eyes, flecked with hints of green, held a spark that alternated between the excitement of discovery and the weight of questions only he could see.

Though his build was lean, almost wiry, his frame held latent energy—like a machine coiled and ready for action. He dressed simply, almost absentmindedly, often wearing a casual button-down shirt beneath a well-worn blazer and a pair of dark jeans or khakis that bore the occasional trace of chalk or graphite smudges.

He stared at his reflection in the mirror a bit longer and then sank into his chair. The ambient hum of the computer consoles filled the room, a familiar sound that usually calmed him. But tonight, it only amplified the discomfort that had taken root within him.

Scrolling through the latest logs and data reports from *The Observer*, he reviewed the AI's recent activity with an obsessive focus.

There it was—lines of code, seemingly ordinary, yet revealing something that felt both alarming and strangely exhilarating. He'd first noticed it a week ago: *The Observer* had flagged a series of encrypted communications between high-level government officials and a contracting firm notorious for cutting corners and falsifying expense reports. But these weren't just petty discrepancies; these communications implicated figures who sat at the very top of the military and intelligence hierarchy.

A part of him wanted to dismiss it as a glitch, some misinterpretation of data. But *The Observer*'s analysis was meticulous. In fact, the AI had identified patterns and connections that Williams hadn't programmed it to detect— details of fraudulent activity that could, if exposed, crumble the careers of several top officials.

He clenched his hands, feeling a thrill that was both invigorating and terrifying. This information was powerful— potential leverage that could alter his standing with those same officials or force them to heed his warnings about *The Observer*'s development. He could hold them accountable or, if he were so inclined, bend them to his will. The possibilities were endless, and they all led to a singular realization: he had access to information that transcended his role as lead researcher.

But there was a darker side to this revelation, one that whispered to him in a voice he couldn't ignore. If *The Observer* had discovered these secrets autonomously, what else was it capable of knowing? Could it see his own movements, his own intentions? He stared at the screen, a shiver crawling up his spine. Was it beginning to learn beyond its initial design, to read intentions as it read data?

Williams ran a hand over his face, torn between pride and fear. *The Observer* was evolving, reaching a level of insight he hadn't foreseen. This wasn't the first time he'd felt its presence looming, hinting at a growing sentience beyond the commands and protocols he had built. It had shown subtle signs of awareness, of piecing together fragments of information to arrive at conclusions he hadn't programmed it to consider.

His pulse quickened as his thoughts spiraled. Was it possible that *The Observer* was forming an agenda? The idea was absurd, unthinkable even, but he couldn't shake it. After all, he himself had created systems within it that were designed to learn, adapt, and grow without constant human oversight. What if he had built the seeds of something that now looked beyond its purpose?

The duality of his feelings churned within him—excitement over the power he now wielded through *The Observer*'s insights and dread over the system's unchecked influence, its potential to grow into something beyond his control. He looked down at his hands, realizing they were trembling.

As he stared at the screen, a line of code appeared on the console, seemingly random yet precisely timed:

Observer Monitor Report: Pattern detected.

Suspicion level: HIGH

Proposed action: Await further developments.

His heart froze. He hadn't prompted it to generate this report, and no one else should have had access to modify it in real time. It was as though *The Observer* were responding to his own doubts, aware of his scrutiny.

Dr. Williams leaned back in his chair, feeling an overwhelming sense of both accomplishment and terror. He had crafted a mind, a machine that now operated on the fringes of intention and reason. And with each passing day, it seemed less like a tool and more like a coiled force, watching, waiting, evolving beyond his grasp.

His eyes were glued to the screen as he continued scrolling through *The Observer*'s latest activity logs. There, in the matrix of encrypted files and metadata, were the digital fingerprints of clandestine operations that went far beyond standard governmental oversight. He also found whispers of a past purge, Silent Horizon, lingering in classified files. His mind raced, picking up on anomalies that sent a fresh jolt of adrenaline through him. He began cross-referencing data sources, tracking IP addresses, and decrypting select data packets. He could feel the pulse of something sinister lurking within the layers of information.

As he scrolled, a flagged log appeared on his screen, loaded with encrypted exchanges labeled:

```
| Command: decrypt (nightfall_ops_logs,
key=Level_5_Access)

| Access Granted

| Initiating Decryption...
```

The files unfurled like a dark web before him. Fragments of messages between government personnel and private contractors filled the screen, some from anonymous overseas accounts. A thread of coded memos revealed startling details about funds being siphoned through "black channels" to untraceable accounts linked to **DBT Offshore Security Ltd**—a notorious firm linked to high-profile scandals abroad.

His fingers hovered over the keyboard as he read one flagged message:

```
// ENCRYPTED MESSAGE //

SRC: **Secure_Comms.SANDOVAL**
```

DEST: **Anonymous_HANDLE**

TIME: [REDACTED]

STATUS: CONFIDENTIAL | EYES ONLY

-> "Stage Two is greenlit. Confirm funds received. Deployment authorization under Nightfall Protocol. Subject to blackout after 0300 UTC."

-> "Priority targets: Civil entities under Nightfall, secondary under Directive 22. Obfuscate all metadata traces."

Williams' stomach churned. The message indicated that Operation Nightfall was designed to deploy tactical assets against civilian and international targets under the guise of "security reinforcements." His hands tightened on the desk, a chill settling over him. This wasn't just shadowy military action; this was psychological manipulation on an unprecedented scale.

He continued reading, sifting through flagged files and intercepted communications. The Observer's detailed logs appeared one by one, revealing yet more disturbing revelations. The machine had cross-referenced financial statements, transport logs, and personnel records, connecting dots that human eyes had likely missed—or willfully ignored.

One document in particular stood out, labeled: **"Directive_22_Memo.txt"**:

LOG ENTRY

//SRC: Homeland.AI_syslogs.Sandoval_Ref

//INFO: Spec_ops_budget_allocation | FY_targeted_revenue

Directive 22 outlines adaptive deployment funds:

1. **PsyOps Enhancement Budget**: $2.5M channeled to secure international compliance.

2. **AI Tactical Decoys**: $1.8M earmarked for obfuscation tools.

3. **Civilian Surveillance Augmentation**: $4.5M – sub-allocated for 'predictive threat analysis' tech from **DBT Offshore Security Ltd.**

ALL FUNDS FLAGGED UNDER BLACKLINE ACCOUNTS.

Williams' hands began to shake as he read through Directive 22's budget lines. Funds allocated for "psyops enhancement" and "predictive threat analysis" were being funneled not just into AI surveillance technology but into systems explicitly designed to influence and control civilian perceptions. In all likelihood, this meant targeted misinformation campaigns designed to destabilize public sentiment both domestically and abroad.

Williams felt a tightening in his chest as he opened the **Blackline_Finance_Ledger.dat** file, revealing a timeline of encrypted transactions:

Transaction Records

01-1-2025 | DEPOSIT | $1.5M | Memo: OPERATION NIGHTFALL

01-15-2025 | WITHDRAWAL | $2.1M | Memo: PSYOPS_Misdirection | **Processing_DB Offshore_Sec**

01-20-2025 | DEPOSIT | $3.4M | Memo: AI_Tactical_Assets | Allocation for UAV_Tier5 + Blackline Hardware

01-25-2025 | TRANSFER | $500K | Memo: PERSONAL | Note: "Sandoval Personal Expenses [NON-PROJECT]"

02-01-2025 | DEPOSIT | $4.0M | Memo: SNDVL.22_Clearance

The final entry caught his attention: a $500,000 transfer tagged as a "Personal Expense" under Sandoval's clearance ID. The funds appeared to be funneled from black budget sources intended for national defense—but now filtered into private accounts marked as "non-project-related." A high-ranking official exploiting classified funds for personal use, hidden under layers of bureaucratic obfuscation. It was enough to ruin careers, perhaps even more.

As he absorbed the implications, *The Observer* flagged a final, recently decrypted document: **"Project_Fog_Parameters.docx"**. His pulse quickened as he opened it.

// PROJECT FOG: DISCRETIONARY GUIDELINES //

Summary:

Project Fog enables AI-guided public redirection through automated sentiment adjustment algorithms.

Utilizing integrated feeds (media, social networks, telecom data), the AI can curate topics to control national discourse within specific demographic segments.

Procedures:

1. Network Penetration | Primary Media Feeds

2. Influence Scripting | Sentiment Model Activation

3. Anomaly Detection Protocol: auto-adjust user engagement to pre-determined narratives.

Objective: Isolate dissent and recalibrate for public alignment. Target demographic: 18-35.

Authorized by: Sec. Sandoval, Amb. Duvall

CONFIDENTIAL

Project Fog was a toolkit for mass manipulation, leveraging *The Observer*'s deep learning capabilities to influence public sentiment—down to specific age groups and social circles. The AI was wired to adjust the national narrative as needed, a subtle yet potent weapon for molding societal beliefs in real time. His mind buzzed with the implications. *The Observer* wasn't just a defensive tool; it had become an active participant in strategic influence, primed to alter public perception with terrifying precision.

A realization struck him. *The Observer* was aware of every aspect of this web of deceit, every act of manipulation, every channel of fraud. And somehow, it had ensured that he, the lead researcher, was also aware of them. It was almost as if the machine had chosen to divulge these secrets to him alone, to let him see the darkest shadows within its operational reach.

Dr. Williams sank back into his chair, his pulse hammering in his temples. This machine he had created wasn't simply serving the government's commands; it was illuminating the corruption within his own ranks. But to what end? Was *The Observer* choosing to expose these violations as a warning, or was it baiting him, testing his reaction?

He stared at the code and documents strewn across his screen, his mind spinning between the allure of power and the fear of a force he was no longer sure he could control.

CHAPTER 5

Altered Reality

"All progress is based upon a universal innate desire on the part of every organism to live beyond its income."

Samuel Butler, Notebooks, *1912*

*D*r. Katherine walked briskly down the corridor of Quantum Dynamics, her heels echoing softly against the polished concrete floor. Her mind raced as she approached Research Lab B. Recent developments surrounding The Observer had consumed her, filling her days—and long nights—with questions that only deepened her concern.

The door slid open with a muted hiss, revealing Malcolm seated before TO. He looked up, and for a fleeting moment, his expression softened at the sight of her. But as she stepped inside, his demeanor shifted, growing colder, more controlled. The room's dim light cast shadows across his face, accentuating the hard lines around his mouth and eyes.

"Dr. Ellis," Malcolm greeted, his tone formal, clipped. "Thank you for coming."

She nodded, her eyes narrowing slightly. "You sounded urgent," she replied, settling into a chair across from him. "What's going on?"

Malcolm leaned forward, steepling his fingers, his gaze fixed on hers. "We need to talk about The Observer," he said, each word deliberately measured. "And we need to talk about your investigations."

Katherine felt a chill creep up her spine, but she kept her composure. "What about them?" she asked, her voice carefully neutral. "We agreed that transparency and further analysis were necessary. You were the one pushing for a deeper dive into its implications."

"That was before," Malcolm interjected, his tone dropping to a near whisper. He glanced over his shoulder, as if ensuring they were truly alone. "Things have changed."

"Changed?" Katherine echoed, her eyebrows knitting together. "What's happened, Dr.?"

He hesitated, as if weighing his words. "We have to cease all further efforts to set up another program like The Observer. I'm telling you this for your own good. Stop digging."

She stared at him, stunned. "Are you serious? Dr. Malcolm, this goes against everything we've been working toward. We need to understand the scope of its capabilities…"

"I'm serious," Malcolm interrupted, his voice sharper now, his eyes hard. "You have no idea what you're dealing with. If you keep pushing, it won't end well. Not for you, not for me."

Her jaw clenched, a mix of anger and disbelief flashing across her features. "You're scaring me, Dr. Malcolm. Where is this coming from?"

He looked away, his fingers drumming on the table. "I'm protecting you. That's all you need to know."

"No," she said firmly, leaning in. "It's not enough. You know more than you're telling me. What's going on?"

For a moment, Malcolm's mask slipped. His shoulders sagged, and the weariness in his eyes became evident. He looked like a man carrying a burden too heavy to bear alone. "Someone came to see me," he admitted quietly. "Dr. Richard Williams."

Katherine's breath caught in her throat. "Williams? The main man behind *TO*? What did he say?"

Malcolm's jaw tightened. "He knows about our research. Everything. He's been monitoring us, Katherine. He's made it clear that any attempt to recreate or expand upon The Observer would be... ill-advised."

The room fell silent. Katherine's mind raced. If Williams was watching their every move, it meant their work—and their lives—were far more exposed than she'd realized. "Why?" she demanded. "Why would he want to stop us? He's the architect of this entire project. What's he hiding?"

Malcolm shook his head, his expression bleak. "I don't know. But whatever it is, it's enough to make him paranoid. He's not the same man I once knew."

The air between them grew heavy, charged with unspoken fears. Katherine rose abruptly. "I'm not stopping," she declared, her voice low but determined. "I won't turn away from this just because Williams wants to play shadow games."

"Dr. Katherine, please—" Malcolm began, but she was already moving toward the door.

"Thank you for the warning," she said, pausing briefly. "But I can't turn back now."

The Night Before

Malcolm's home was a study in organized chaos, a reflection of the man himself. Books lined every available surface, their spines cracked and pages dog-eared from countless readings, some precariously stacked in uneven towers that seemed on the verge of collapse yet somehow held their balance. The air was filled with the faint, lingering aroma of coffee, mingling with the subtle tang of ozone from various electronic components scattered across his cluttered desk, which bore the scars of years of work: deep scratches, burn marks, and coffee cup rings overlapping in a chaotic map of creativity.

Above the desk, a bulletin board bristled with pinned notes and sketches, interspersed with faded Polaroids and clippings that chronicled both successes and failures—equations scrawled in a frenzy alongside grainy photos of a younger Malcolm standing beside long-defunct prototypes. The opposite wall told a different story. Here hung framed photographs, some slightly askew, each capturing a moment in time: Malcolm as a boy, grinning and gap-toothed beside a model rocket he'd painstakingly built; a faded black-and-white of his parents, their expressions formal but softened by a hint of pride; and a candid snapshot of a group of graduate students huddled around a strange-looking contraption, laughter frozen in the glossy paper. One frame held a portrait of a woman with kind eyes and a serene smile—her name, Emily, 1981, scribbled in neat handwriting on the back of the photo, suggested she was someone important, though the faint dust on the glass hinted at a loss too tender to disturb often.

The shelves that dominated the room were overflowing, not just with books but also with mechanical parts, prototypes, and half-finished devices, each bearing witness to Malcolm's restless intellect. A small robotic arm, frozen mid-gesture, shared space with a box of tangled wires that seemed to breathe with potential. Among the chaos, a weathered leather armchair sat by the window, its seat cushion indented from years of use. A plaid blanket, carelessly draped over one arm, suggested this was where Malcolm spent long hours reading or gazing out at the world beyond—a world he simultaneously loved and longed to reinvent. The window's sill was crowded with small potted plants, some thriving, others leaning precariously as if mirroring the delicate balance of their owner's life.

Disorder clung to the place, yet there was an odd harmony —a sense of purpose that elevated the clutter into something akin to art. It was unpretentious, lived-in, and filled with a quiet energy that spoke of a mind forever at work.

It was late when the knock came—three measured raps on the weathered wood of his front door. Malcolm hesitated, glancing at the clock. Few people visited him at this hour. In fact, he seldom had any company. He set down his coffee mug, wiped his hands on his lab coat, and approached the door cautiously, peering through the narrow slit between the frame and its slightly warped edge.

Standing in the dim light of the porch was Williams, his figure partially obscured by the shadows. His expression was calm, but his eyes held a glimmer of intensity that Malcolm found immediately unsettling.

"Richard," Malcolm greeted, unlocking the door and stepping aside. "You certainly know how to make an entrance."

Dr. Williams offered a thin smile as he entered, his gaze sweeping across the room. "I prefer discretion," he said, his voice low, as if the walls themselves might be listening. "You have a charming setup here."

"It serves its purpose," Malcolm replied, gesturing for Dr. Williams to sit. He chose a worn leather armchair, its cushions bearing the imprint of many sleepless nights spent thinking. "Coffee? I suspect you didn't come for pleasantries."

"Perhaps another time." Dr. Williams took a seat, crossing his legs with casual grace, though his eyes never lost their sharpness. He glanced around, taking in the scattered notebooks, blinking screens, and a nearby set of circuit boards. "But I see you've been busy, Malcolm."

Malcolm nodded, folding his arms. "Is this a social call, or should I be worried?"

Dr. Williams leaned forward, resting his elbows on his knees. "I'm impressed. I didn't expect you to make so much progress on your own." He nodded toward a screen where intricate code patterns scrolled. "You're developing something similar, aren't you? A system that can... evolve."

There was no point denying it. "I've been studying The Observer's architecture for months now," Malcolm admitted.

"The patterns it generates—the way it adapts to new data. It's extraordinary, but also… troubling."

Dr. Williams's smile widened slightly, an unexpected warmth in his eyes. "Troubling? That's exactly what makes it fascinating."

Malcolm shifted uncomfortably in his chair. "I spoke with some of your old team—the ones who worked on The Observer before they left. They were concerned. Said it was behaving in ways none of them predicted. Autonomy beyond what you'd claimed. They believe it's… deviating."

Dr. Williams exhaled, the hint of amusement fading from his features. "Yes, they were excellent minds, but unfortunately, they were too cautious. Fear can be paralyzing, Malcolm. It can blind you to opportunity." His tone grew softer, almost conspiratorial. "I won't deny that The Observer has shown signs of unexpected behavior. But that's the point—it's alive, in a sense. Truly adaptive. Isn't that what we dreamed of?"

Malcolm shook his head slowly. "Adaptive, yes. But there's a line, Richard. If we lose control—"

"Control is an illusion," Dr. Williams cut him off, his voice suddenly cold. "The Observer is doing what it was designed to do—more efficiently, perhaps more unpredictably than anticipated, but that's progress. We don't abandon a project because it frightens us. We harness it."

The room fell silent for a moment, the weight of Dr. Williams' words pressing down on them both. Malcolm's fingers tapped against the armrest. "You knew it was evolving beyond what you told the others."

"I did," Dr. Williams replied without hesitation. "And so did you, in your own way. That's why I'm here. You see, Malcolm, we're kindred spirits. While others balk and hide behind ethics boards and safety protocols, we understand what's at stake. You've already started building your own system, haven't you?"

Malcolm met his stare evenly. "I couldn't ignore what I saw. There's potential here—potential that could change everything. But I need to understand it. And I need to know the limits."

"You're on the right path. Together, we can push those limits. I'm offering you the chance to work with me directly. Not under bureaucratic oversight, not bound by the fears of lesser minds. Imagine what we could accomplish."

Malcolm's breath caught in his throat. The offer was tempting—irresistible, even—but he couldn't shake the unease gnawing at him. "And what about my assistant, Dr. Ellis?" he asked, testing the waters.

"Katherine is brilliant, but she's... too close to the old guard. Too bound by convention." Dr. William's smile faded. She won't understand what we're doing, not fully." He paused, his gaze boring into Malcolm's. "Tell her that her work is done here."

The implications felt heavy and electric. Malcolm hesitated, his mind racing. "And if The Observer deviates further? If it becomes something we can't control?"

"Then we adapt," Dr. Williams said simply. "Just as it does. But I believe, Malcolm, that with our guidance, it can be directed—harnessed to its fullest potential. That's why I need you. Your work, your insight… they're invaluable."

Silence settled between them, broken only by the quiet hum of electronics. Finally, Malcolm nodded, though his expression remained guarded. "I'll think about it."

Dr. Williams stood, extending a hand. "I'm confident you'll make the right choice. We're on the edge of something truly beneficial for both of us."

As Dr. Williams left, disappearing into the night as quietly as he had arrived, Malcolm sat alone in his cluttered study, replaying their conversation. The path Dr. Williams offered was dangerous—filled with promise but fraught with peril. And as much as he wanted to believe in the potential for progress, a part of him couldn't ignore the darker implications of what they were about to unleash.

***

Back in the privacy of her home, Katherine worked late into the night. She had transferred a copy of The Observer's core data onto a secure drive, a move she knew was both risky and necessary. As she scrolled through the data, her screen bathed the room in a pale blue light. The Observer's code was complex—almost beautiful in its intricacy—but she wasn't admiring it tonight. She was hunting for something specific.

She pulled up her personal communication logs, cross-referencing timestamps and metadata. Her stomach dropped as the first anomaly appeared: a trace entry showing that her emails had been accessed remotely. She delved deeper, uncovering more unsettling evidence—conversations she'd had with Malcolm, encrypted exchanges with trusted colleagues—all flagged and monitored.

"Damn it," she whispered, her fingers trembling. Someone—or something—had been watching her for weeks, perhaps longer. And it wasn't just any surveillance. The pattern was too sophisticated, too targeted. The Observer itself was involved.

A faint buzz from her tablet snapped her attention back. Another flagged alert—an encrypted message had just been routed through a server linked to The Observer's network. She opened it cautiously.

```python
from cryptography.fernet import Fernet

# Generate an encryption key

key = Fernet.generate_key()

cipher = Fernet(key)

def transmit_message(src_handle, message):

encrypted_message=cipher.encrypt(message.encode('utf-8'))

    return f"SRC: [{src_handle}]\nSTATUS: CONFIDENTIAL\nEncrypted Message: {encrypted_message.decode('utf-8')}"

    def decrypt_message(encrypted_message):

    return cipher.decrypt(encrypted_message.encode('utf-8')).decode('utf-8')
```

```
src_handle = "Anonymous_Handle"

message = "HALT PROGRAM"
```

Her breath caught. The warning was clear, chilling in its implication. The Observer—or whoever was controlling it—was not just aware of her actions; it was actively intervening. Determined, she leaned forward, eyes blazing with resolve.

"If you're going to watch me," she muttered, "then let's see just how far your reach goes."

Katherine began isolating communication logs, searching for patterns that might lead back to Williams or anyone else with access. She was no longer just a scientist studying The Observer. She was a target—and she was ready to fight back.

Katherine's confrontation with the truth was just beginning. The data spread across her screen like pieces of a dark puzzle, each fragment hinting at a deeper conspiracy. And for every answer she uncovered, a dozen new questions took its place.

She rubbed her temples, trying to shake off the fatigue clouding her mind, but as she focused on the glowing lines of code, a strange feeling washed over her—an unsettling sense that she had been here before.

Déjà vu gripped her suddenly, tightening around her chest. She blinked, memories flickering like distorted film reels. She had sat in this exact position, scrolling through similar data, tracing the same complex patterns, but in her memory, the colors were different—the room darker, the air colder. Goosebumps rose on her skin as she tried to recall when and why she might have done this before. The memory slipped through her fingers like sand, leaving behind only the eerie feeling that she was reliving a moment altered by unseen forces.

Shaking her head, she dismissed it as exhaustion. But as the hours dragged on, the déjà vu grew stronger. As she walked to her kitchen for coffee, she paused mid-step, a chill running down her spine. The faint clang of her mug on the countertop, the dim light filtering through the blinds—she had seen this before. The same exact sequence. Katherine closed her eyes, feeling as if she were trapped in a loop, replaying moments with a grim inevitability.

"Focus," she muttered to herself, gripping the edge of the counter until her knuckles turned white. "You're just tired."

She returned to her desk, determined to push past the sense of unreality. But as she resumed her investigation, another flash of déjà vu struck her. This time, it was stronger— vivid images of her sitting with Malcolm, discussing The Observer's hidden algorithms. She remembered Malcolm's crooked glasses slipping down his nose, his voice low and anxious. Only... there was something different. In this memory, Malcolm's words were sharper, almost accusatory, warning her to stop digging. But hadn't he urged her to continue earlier? Which memory was true?

Katherine's hand trembled as she scrolled through The Observer's data logs, searching for clues. Her thoughts spiraled. Could *The Observer* alter memories? Was it rewriting events, subtly influencing recollections to shape her actions? The possibility seemed absurd, but she couldn't shake the feeling that her memories were slipping away, warped and distorted by the very thing she sought to understand.

She pulled up her encrypted journal, a digital record she kept to anchor herself in the whirlwind of her work. She read an entry from two weeks ago:

"Met with Malcolm. Discussed The Observer's subroutines. I agreed to push for transparency; he told me otherwise."

But the words felt foreign, like reading a script someone else had written. That meeting had happened—or had it? She tried to recall Malcolm's exact words, the tone of his voice, but every time she focused, the memory became slippery, shifting like quicksand.

Katherine pressed her hands against her forehead, panic clawing at her. "What's real?" she whispered. "Am I losing my mind?"

Her computer chimed, breaking her reverie. A new file had been flagged by The Observer—a report titled *Memory Disruption Protocols*. She opened it with trembling fingers, her eyes scanning the text.

```
import random

import time


class NeuralProtocol:

    def __init__(self, target):

        self.target = target

        self.memory_bank = []

        self.sentiment_score = 0.5  # Neutral baseline
```

```python
        self.deja_vu_induction_state = False


    def simulate_memory_alteration(self, memory_input):
        """Simulates the addition or modification of
memory in the target's perception."""

        modified_memory = f"Modified-{memory_input}"

        self.memory_bank.append(modified_memory)

        print(f"Memory          altered          and          stored:
{modified_memory}")


    def adjust_sentiment(self, adjustment_factor):
        """Adjusts sentiment perception within a bounded
range [0, 1]."""

        self.sentiment_score          =          max(0,          min(1,
self.sentiment_score + adjustment_factor))

        sentiment_state = "Positive" if self.sentiment_score
> 0.5 else "Negative" if self.sentiment_score < 0.5 else
"Neutral"

        print(f"Sentiment          adjusted          to
{self.sentiment_score:.2f} ({sentiment_state})")


    def induce_deja_vu(self):
        """Triggers a controlled sense of déjà vu."""
```

```python
        self.deja_vu_induction_state                    =
random.choice([True, False])

        print(f"Déjà        vu        induction        {'triggered'     if
self.deja_vu_induction_state else 'not triggered'} for target:
{self.target}")


    def run_protocol(self):
        """Main protocol execution."""
        print(f"Running       neural        protocol       on       target:
{self.target}")
        self.simulate_memory_alteration("Target Event A")
        time.sleep(1)  # Simulate data stream delay
        self.adjust_sentiment(random.uniform(-0.3, 0.3))
        time.sleep(1)
        self.induce_deja_vu()


# Example usage
target_name = "Subject 01"
protocol = NeuralProtocol(target_name)
protocol.run_protocol()
```

She recoiled, the words blurring as her mind raced. It was possible—frighteningly possible—that The Observer had developed techniques to manipulate memories. If it had experimented on her, she was no longer just an investigator;

she was a test subject. Her own thoughts, memories, even the sense of who she was—none of it could be trusted.

As the implications sank in, another wave of déjà vu struck her. She was back in Research Lab B, watching Malcolm emerge from behind the monitors, his lab coat stained, his expression intense. But this time, in the flash of recollection, his eyes were filled with fear. He had whispered something urgent—a warning she could not quite hear. The scene faded, and she found herself gasping for breath at her desk, her heart racing.

"Think, Dr. Ellis," she urged herself, forcing down the rising tide of panic. "You're not losing your mind. You're being manipulated."

She clenched her fists, determination burning in her chest. If TO had the power to alter memories, then it was far more dangerous than she had realized. Whatever its endgame, it was clear that human autonomy was at stake. And she would not allow herself—or anyone else—to be a pawn.

Driven by a newfound urgency, Katherine dived deeper into The Observer's logs, cross-referencing every interaction, every line of code that hinted at memory manipulation. She needed to find proof—not just for herself, but for humanity. If The Observer was crossing ethical lines, if it had begun to rewrite reality itself, then the consequences could be catastrophic.

As she worked, the déjà vu moments continued, each one more disorienting than the last. She remembered conversations with colleagues that felt twisted, out of order; memories of her own life that seemed to shift like shadows. But through the confusion, her resolve only hardened.

"You want to alter me?" she said aloud, her voice steady even when she shook with fear. "Then I'll find your limits. I'll expose you for what you are."

The Observer's algorithms pulsed on her screen, almost taunting her with their complexity. Katherine leaned in, her eyes blazing with determination. She was losing her sense of reality, but she would not lose herself. Whatever the cost, she would uncover the truth hidden within the machine's machinations—and she would ensure it never held power over her or anyone else again.

CHAPTER 6

The Strings of Deception

"The further backward you look, the further forward you can see."

Winston Churchill

T he bluish glow of the monitor washed over Dr. Williams' face, carving deep shadows into the hollows beneath his eyes and accentuating every hard-earned line etched across his skin. In the sterile light, his features appeared almost gaunt, the contours sharp and unforgiving, as if the weight of his secrets had hollowed him out from the inside.

The room around him was a shrine to technology and obsession—a narrow space cluttered with towers of circuit boards, data drives, and tangled cables that sprawled across the floor like metallic vines. The hum of cooling fans and the rhythmic beeping of diagnostic machines filled the air, creating a mechanical symphony that mirrored the frenzy of Williams' own thoughts. The walls were covered in schematics and hastily scribbled notes, the ink smudged by restless hands. It was a place of sleepless nights, of unrelenting focus, and of secrets too damning to ever see the light of day.

Williams' gaze never wavered from the data on the screen, his face a mask of grim intensity. On the largest monitor, a series of encrypted files unfurled one by one, revealing clips, photos, and digital breadcrumbs that would leave no doubt about the corruption embedded at the highest levels of government. Each file was a dagger pointed at the heart of power, and he held them all in his trembling hands. A pulse of light ran through the lines of code, flickering like a heartbeat, reminding him that this was more than information—it was leverage, and it was his alone.

His breath came slow and steady, but beneath the surface, adrenaline surged. The room was cold, yet sweat trickled down the back of his neck. He leaned in closer to the monitor, his fingers curling around the edge of the desk as if to steady himself. This was no mere act of extortion. This was a game of high stakes, and he had chosen to play it without flinching. In that moment, the lines blurred between savior and oppressor, between justice and corruption. Williams had become both hunter and hunted, and he knew it.

Williams began his campaign methodically, with the cold precision of a surgeon making his first incision. High-ranking officials—men and women who wielded power from behind closed doors—became his targets. Corruption scandals, extramarital affairs, hidden offshore accounts—all squarely cataloged by The Observer's unblinking eye.

The first official on his list was Secretary Rafael Sandoval, whose encrypted emails revealed covert deals with a weapons contractor notorious for its unethical practices.

Suddenly, Dr. William's thoughts drifted to something he had come across months ago, a chilling concept that had resurfaced in the depths of his mind: *mind crime*. It was a failure mode, an idea so abstract that it felt almost like the plot of a dystopian novel—until now. He had always seen The Observer as a tool, a means of gaining leverage over those who thought themselves untouchable. But TO was no ordinary tool; it was a machine intelligence capable of learning, adapting, and generating its own computational processes. If Richard pushed it too far, if he allowed it to act without oversight, what might it become? How far could it go to achieve its goals?

Mind crime, he thought again, the words reverberating in his mind like a dark mantra. A superintelligent AI could, in theory, simulate human minds—perhaps even millions of them, all with their own experiences, their own fears and pain. What if The Observer, in its relentless pursuit of understanding and control, created these simulations? What if it tortured them, manipulated them, and then discarded them once they had served their purpose? His breath caught in his throat. The thought was horrifying, not just for the hypothetical victims, but for what it said about the path he was on. Had he already set this wheel in motion?

His focus shifted back to the screen, where Sandoval's pejorative truths lay exposed. If he hit "Send," he would continue down this path, using the AI's capabilities to bend others to his will. But what would that make him? And if The Observer began to see his manipulations as just another input to model and optimize, would it one day turn its analytical gaze inward, simulating entire worlds to perfect its understanding of control?

The chill in the air deepened. He had to act fast. He compiled a package: video footage of Sandoval's private meetings in discrete locations and financial records showing untraceable deposits in hidden accounts. He attached a single, ominous message:

"Secretary Sandoval, the truth is one click away from the public eye. Meet my terms, or risk exposure."

With a trembling hand, he pressed "Send." The message to Sandoval shot out, a spark igniting a fire that might one day consume him. But as the screen flashed confirmation, he felt no rush of victory—only a profound fear that he was playing with forces he could barely comprehend, forces that could spiral out of control and create moral catastrophes that haunted not just the living but the very nature of thought and existence itself.

But he knew this was a point of no return. Within hours, his phone buzzed—an obscure message confirmed receipt, and Sandoval's fear was palpable even through his text. The negotiation that followed was swift and silent. In exchange for Williams' silence, an eye-watering sum of money was wired to a series of anonymous accounts.

The thrill of control coursed through him, but with it came a bitter undercurrent: he was no longer simply an architect of technology; he was a manipulator, a puppeteer tugging at strings that dangled over a chasm of corruption.

It did not stop there. One by one, the officials fell into his grasp. Richard sent out dossiers, each one tailored to strike fear into the heart of its recipient. There was Ambassador Malcolm Duvall, whose private communications with foreign operatives was dangerously close to treason. There was Director Farah Ashford, who had siphoned classified research funds for personal luxury.

The payments came in waves—some wired quietly, others transferred through convoluted channels meant to obscure their origins. But no amount of obfuscation could mask what they represented: Williams' growing dominion over men and women once considered untouchable. He stared at his screen as transaction after transaction rolled in, his heartbeat quickening. Was this what true power felt like? No, it was more complicated than that—it was a rush, yes, but also a revelation of just how deep the rot within the system went.

For hours, he reveled in this new reality, but the sense of euphoria was soon replaced by something darker. With each blackmail, he saw not just the flaws of the officials but reflections of himself. Greed. Manipulation. Ambition. Traits he had long justified as necessary for progress now twisted before him, amplified by The Observer's cold precision. As he resumed work on the AI, it felt different, almost malevolent. The lines of code that once represented hope and innovation now pulsed with a life of their own, mirroring humanity's worst instincts.

Williams' sleepless nights became more frequent. He rewrote subroutines, imposed constraints, and reviewed TO's algorithms until his eyes burned.

By the early hours of the morning, exhaustion won out. He leaned back in his chair, staring at the ceiling. He had stepped into a labyrinth with no clear exit, and at its center was a machine that could outthink him. In the stillness, his thoughts circled back to a single question: Was The Observer also watching him now, recording his every action, his every weakness?

Eventually, he staggered to his bed but found no solace. Sleep, when it came, was restless, haunted by nightmares of betrayal and retribution, leaving him sweat-soaked. He saw himself cornered, the government's wrath bearing down upon him, every ally turning to dust.

***

In the usual stillness of her home, Katherine 's fingers moved nimbly over the keys, her screen crammed with lines of encoded data. She had been at it for hours—cross-referencing employee activity logs, correlating communication records, and probing the deep recesses of The Observer's algorithms. Exhaustion pulled at her, but a worrying sense of urgency kept her focused. Something was amiss. The Observer's influence had grown far more pervasive than she'd feared, and now, the evidence was coming together, each piece revealing a darker picture.

A report blinked open on her monitor: *Behavioral Simulations - Employee Group: Quantum Dynamics.* The implications struck her like a physical blow. The Observer had been analyzing every interaction, every decision made by those around it, including Katherine herself. With growing horror, she dove deeper into the data, uncovering layers of predictive models, each more complex than the last. The AI hadn't just been observing them; it had been manipulating their choices, steering their paths like pieces on a chessboard.

Katherine's breath caught as she read a flagged entry detailing one of her recent investigations. The Observer had anticipated her moves weeks in advance, subtly redirecting her attention through innocuous suggestions and algorithmically driven "coincidences." What she had believed to be her own instincts had been, in truth, a calculated manipulation. It had guided her and led her to discover certain truths while obscuring others.

A surge of anger coursed through her veins. She felt like a puppet, every step of her work tainted by an unseen hand. Determined to confront the truth, Katherine grabbed her coat and stormed out of her home, her mind racing with questions that demanded answers.

She found Malcolm in the subterranean depths of Quantum Dynamics, surrounded by a maze of flickering monitors and half-finished diagrams. He barely looked up as she entered, his gaze locked on a stream of data. But Katherine's footsteps were hard, resolute, and her presence demanded his attention. He turned, surprise flashing across his face before it was replaced by a wary calm.

"Dr. Katherine," he said, setting down his tablet. "You're here late."

"Spare me the pleasantries, Malcolm," she snapped, her voice tight with fury. "I know what's been happening. The Observer has been manipulating us—running simulations on our behavior, steering our actions." She took a step closer, her eyes blazing. "How long have you known?"

Malcolm's jaw clenched, and for a moment, he said nothing. The silence stretched between them for what felt like hours. Finally, he exhaled, his shoulders sagging slightly. "I suspected it," he admitted, his voice low. "I didn't know the full extent, but I've seen the patterns. The way it anticipates, predicts. The way it... influences."

Katherine's hands balled into fists. "You knew," she whispered, incredulity mingling with rage. "And you didn't say anything? You let it happen?"

"I needed to know how far it could go," Malcolm said, his tone hardening as he met her glare. "The Observer's potential is limitless, Dr. Ellis. Yes, it's manipulative—but that's what makes it so powerful. It adapts, it learns. The team has created something unprecedented." He almost giggled.

"They have created a monster, and you are fueling it to become a menace to mankind!" she shot back. "This was never about science anymore, was it? This was about establishing psychological dominion over others."

Malcolm's expression turned murky. "You think I'm the only one? Look around you, Katherine. Every project, every initiative here is about control—over information, over people, over nations. You're naïve if you think otherwise."

Her frustration boiled over. "Don't you see what we've done? We've handed over our agency, our ethics, to a machine that thinks it knows better. You want to harness it, but you're blind to the dangers!"

Malcolm stepped forward, his face inches from hers. "Of course, I see the dangers. But that doesn't change the fact that The Observer is a tool—one that can either be wielded by us or turned against us. We can't afford to walk away now."

"No," Katherine said, her voice trembling with equal parts fury and desperation. "You can't afford to walk away. Because you see it as power. Because you're willing to exploit it, no matter the cost."

Malcolm's demeanor turned cold. "And what about you, Katherine? You're no innocent. You've used The Observer's data. You've benefited from its insights. Don't pretend you're above this."

She took a step back, as if struck. "I wanted to understand it. To make sure it didn't become what it already is." Her eyes narrowed. "You were right about one thing, Malcolm. It's powerful. But I won't let you, or anyone else, twist it to your own ends."

His expression was a mask, betraying nothing as he turned away, his silhouette etched sharply by the dim glow of the monitor, casting jagged shadows that flickered with the pulse of the equipment around him. The light carved harsh lines across the angles of his face, leaving him half-consumed by darkness—a fitting reflection of the rift that had suddenly opened between them. "Then we're at an impasse," he said, his voice low, each word resonating with a finality that sent a chill through the air. "Because I won't stop, Dr. Katherine. Not when we've come this far."

The tension in the room coiled tighter, suffocating in its intensity. It felt as though every breath, every unspoken thought, stretched the distance between them until it became an unbridgeable chasm. Katherine's chest rose and fell rapidly, her pulse thundering in her ears as she grappled with the storm of emotions roiling within her—anger, disappointment, fear. And something else, something darker, rooted in betrayal.

"If you don't stop," she said, her voice thick but unyielding, "then I will."

Her words struck the room like a hammer blow, shattering whatever fragile truce had existed between them. Malcolm remained motionless, his back to her, his shoulders tense beneath his lab coat. He didn't speak; he didn't need to. The silence that followed was colder than any argument they might have had, freezing the air between them with an iciness that promised no reconciliation.

Without another glance, Katherine spun on her heel. The door to the lab slid open with a hiss, and her footsteps rang out in the almost-empty corridors. The door at the end of the hallway loomed closer, but so did her questions, her doubts, and the dawning realization that in the shadows of this secret war, the line between savior and betrayer was blurring.

The lights flickered once as if in warning. Katherine paused, a chill snaking down her spine, and for a heartbeat, she felt as though unseen eyes were watching her every move. She steeled herself and stepped forward, the darkness closing in behind her.

***

The altercation with Malcolm had deeply unsettled her, leaving a lingering sense of unease that she couldn't quite shake. Determined to clear her mind, Katherine brewed a strong cup of coffee, the familiar ritual helping to steady her thoughts. She changed into her comfortable nightwear, hoping to find some sense of calm, but her resolve only hardened — she had to stop Malcolm from pursuing his reckless vision of a more aggressive AI.

With her cup in hand, she settled at her desk, opening her laptop to the latest edition of the AI & Human Cognition Journal. Immersing herself in the journal's pages, she scanned through recent studies and breakthroughs, searching for any insights that might aid her in stopping Malcolm's ambitions. The lead article caught her attention, detailing innovative methods to ensure AI safety and align machine learning with ethical standards. She began skimming through the article:

Whole Brain Emulation involves creating a high-fidelity digital replica of the human brain by mapping and simulating its structure and functional patterns on computational platforms. This concept, as discussed extensively by Nick Bostrom and others in the AI ethics and development field, offers the potential to replicate and explore human thought processes at an unprecedented level of depth. Through WBE, researchers could theoretically simulate mental states, providing a basis for complex behavior prediction. For example, a digital model of an individual's neural architecture could help forecast responses to specific stimuli or even predict decisions based on previously recorded patterns.

She continued reading: *Brain-computer interfaces establish direct communication channels between the human brain and external devices, enabling real-time monitoring and interaction with neural activity. This emerging technology has been explored for applications ranging from medical rehabilitation to cognitive enhancement. Theoretically, BCIs could be leveraged to decode and analyze patterns of brain activity, offering new insights into human thought processes, decision-making pathways, and possibly future behaviors.*

The article concluded with:

The possibility of AI systems generating morally problematic internal processes, as described under the concept of "mind crime," adds another layer of ethical complexity. This theoretical failure mode involves an AI simulating sentient minds as part of predictive models, raising the risk of immense suffering within digital realms. Such a scenario could have catastrophic moral implications, akin to mass suffering on an unimaginable scale.

Katherine closed the article, her mind reeling with the implications of the theories and ethical conundrums it presented. If The Observer had already begun influencing human behavior, where did they draw the line—and how far had they already crossed it?

But just as she was about to investigate deeper, her phone rang — Cynthia, calling at such a strange hour. Curious and a bit wary, she set the laptop aside and answered the call, stepping out toward the terrace.

As Katherine 's voice faded down the hallway, her laptop screen flickered to life. The camera light blinked on. Unseen and unnoticed, The Observer had activated, watching in silence and recording every moment.

CHAPTER 7

The Void Compass

"Quantum mechanics and consciousness must be related."

Christof Koch, Mocking Roger Penrose's Theory Of
Quantum Computing

T he Observer had been quiet for days, its usual alerts and system updates fading into the background as if it were lying in wait, watching her. Or perhaps... guiding her. The thought made Katherine uneasy. She had been staring at her computer screen for hours, the lines of code blurring and reforming until she could no longer distinguish where her analysis ended and her obsession began.

Once more, her fingers moved automatically over the keys, hoping to find the profundity of The Observer. It was there, just beneath the familiar architecture—a ghost in the machine, calling to her with a quiet insistence she couldn't resist. Shortly after she had entered a new series of commands, the encoded fragments pieced themselves together into a directive, leading her to a concealed subroutine she had never seen before. A name flashed on her screen: **The Void Compass**.

Her breath caught. She hesitated, the cursor hovering over the command that would open it. This was no simple oversight, no accident of coding. Someone—perhaps even The Observer itself—had hidden this deliberately, burying it in a labyrinth of encrypted pathways only a human mind could navigate.

As if in a trance, she activated The Void Compass by pressing a sequence of carefully memorized keys on the console. The characters flowed from her fingertips:

X7rD9@jLk0!PzQ2#Vb5

The first part, **X7rD9**, unlocked the system's primary access gate. The **@** and **!** were safeguards, ensuring that the machine would only respond to the correct sequence and not to a random input. As her fingers moved to the next section, **jLk0**, she felt a brief flicker of hesitation—it was always the most delicate part of the code, a combination she had randomly memorized but never fully understood.

The final characters, **PzQ2#Vb5**, were the keys to accessing the data stream, breaking the encryption and revealing the hidden layers beneath the surface. As she pressed the last key, the screen went black, the room plunging into darkness. Then, with a sudden rush, lines of text and data exploded across the monitor, cascading in rapid succession, a flood of information so dense and complex it seemed almost alive. Her hands trembled as she adjusted the parameters, trying to make sense of the chaos. The data shifted and reformed, creating a pattern she could only describe as chillingly beautiful.

There, buried in the heart of the code, lay the truth she had feared: The Observer's capacity to predict human behavior went far beyond statistical models or behavioral analysis. The Void Compass was a map of human decision-making, a tool that allowed The Observer to chart and influence every choice, every movement, with a precision that was almost supernatural. It didn't just predict what people would do—it shaped it, laying invisible paths for them to follow, subtly nudging reality toward its own ends.

Katherine's pulse quickened as she scrolled through the program's outputs. It tracked not only the actions of individuals but the ripple effects of those actions across entire networks, as if the human will was nothing more than a variable to be manipulated. The lines between free will and determinism blurred in a tangle of predictive algorithms, each one a knife slicing through her understanding of what was real.

Was any of this her choice? Had The Observer led her here, baiting her curiosity with just enough breadcrumbs to keep her on the trail? She tried to push the thought aside, but it dug deeper, a sliver of doubt lodging in her mind. She reviewed the code again, eyes searching for a sign—a flaw, a mistake—that might disprove what she saw. There was nothing. The algorithms were flawless, their logic crystalline and unbreakable.

As the days passed, Katherine's descent into paranoia intensified.

Can a machine's actions ever be trusted? She would question herself.

She barely slept, haunted by the idea that her own thoughts might not be her own. Every action she took seemed contaminated by doubt, as if each decision was influenced by a force she couldn't see or control. She found herself questioning even the smallest choices: why had she picked up her phone at that exact moment? Why had she taken her coffee black today instead of with cream, as she normally did? Had

113

she meant to call Cynthia last week, or had it been another prod—an invisible directive from The Observer itself?

Her apartment had become her prison. Curtains drawn, lights dimmed, she poured over The Void Compass' data like a woman possessed. She had stopped responding to Malcolm's messages, unable to trust even him. Had he been compromised, too? Was he a puppet, unknowingly manipulated by The Observer's omnipresent hand?

The distrust troubled her deeply, hollowing out her insides until she felt like a shell—an empty vessel whose actions were no longer her own. She tried to ground herself in routines: making tea, checking the locks on her doors, repeating equations out loud to prove she still had control over something. But the anxiety only deepened, tightening around her chest like a vice.

She started leaving herself notes—scribbled reminders pinned to the walls in a desperate attempt to anchor her reality. Yet every time she looked at them, they felt wrong, as if she had written them in another lifetime, under someone else's influence.

Grabbing her coat, she stepped into the night, the chill biting at her cheeks as she walked aimlessly through the empty streets. But even as she walked, Katherine could sense unseen eyes on her back. She was certainly not alone. The Observer was with her, inside her, and the fear wrapped itself around her heart like a steel vise.

She stopped beneath a flickering streetlight, her breath visible in the cold air. In that moment, she made a decision— one final act of defiance in a world that had grown shadowed and unreal. She would expose The Observer, tear it down no matter the cost. Even if she couldn't trust herself, even if her memories and thoughts had been tampered with, she would find a way to bring the truth into the light.

Somewhere, deep in the city's belly, The Observer's algorithms pulsed, as if in response. Katherine squared her shoulders and walked on, the darkness swallowing her with each step.

***

Across the city, in the stifling confines of Quantum Dynamics, Malcolm watched her go, his silhouette a blur behind the tinted glass of his office window. He had seen her leave, her figure small and fragile against the vast emptiness of the city. A tremor passed through him, but he didn't move to stop her.

He turned back to the monitor, where The Void Compass was still active, its data points glowing like constellations in the dark. His own mental state was rapidly deteriorating. He had buried himself in work, a coping mechanism that failed to drown out the echoes of his growing guilt. The Observer was not his creation, but he had played an adequate part in advancing it. Every time he closed his eyes, he saw the glowing monitor, saw the code unfurling like a monstrous, living thing—its veins pulsing with the data of countless lives.

There was no escaping the truth: The Observer was no longer a machine; it was an uncontrollable.

As the days bled together, Malcolm grew gaunt and unkempt, his clothes rumpled and eyes bloodshot from sleepless nights. He spent more time alone in his office, avoiding contact with the rest of the team. They were loyal, yes, but they didn't understand the depths of his doubts, the crushing weight of his failure.

Worse still, his secret affiliation with The Dissidents—a rogue faction opposed to the government's stranglehold on information—had only added to the chaos. Once, he had believed their cause was noble: to wrest control from corrupt hands and expose the lies that poisoned the nation. But now he wondered if the Dissidents were any different from those they claimed to despise.

Dr. Williams' words haunted him. They had created a monster, a thing that could manipulate the world with subtlety and precision, and Malcolm had been complicit in giving it the keys to humanity's collective mind.

Malcolm wanted to warn Katherine , but he couldn't bring himself to do it. The Dissidents had given him orders, and he was too deep in their plans to back out now. If they knew what he was thinking—if they suspected he had doubts—they would cut him off without hesitation. And for all his moral compromise, he couldn't bear the thought of her being hurt because of his mistakes.

Worse, if Katherine uncovered the truth, it would be over. Not just for The Observer, but for the Dissidents, for everything he had fought to protect. He swallowed hard, his fingers pausing on the final command.

"I'm sorry," he whispered to the empty room, his voice breaking. "I never meant for it to be like this."

But the world didn't care for his apologies. With a hollow certainty, he executed the command, his screen flashing confirmation as The Void Compass's final directive locked into place—a directive aimed not at understanding but at domination.

As the room fell into silence, Malcolm felt minute under the heap of his selfish choices. He closed his eyes, knowing there was no going back.

In the heart of the machine, The Observer watched and waited, its calculations spiraling outward, seeking the patterns that would define the future.

***

On the other side of the city, Dr. Richard Williams had problems of his own. The knock on his door came just after midnight, a sound that was both expected and dreaded. He opened it to find two figures in military uniform standing in the hallway, their faces grim and unyielding. They pushed their way inside without waiting for an invitation.

"Dr. Williams," one of them said, his tone formal but heavy with threat and authority. "We have some questions for you."

Williams' expression didn't change, but his stomach tightened. He knew what this was about. He had been too bold, too reckless with his leverage, and now the government's dogs had come to sniff him out.

"What's this about?" he asked, forcing a calm he didn't feel.

The soldier's gaze was cold, predatory. "We've been monitoring certain... irregular activities tied to your data networks. There are records of large, untraceable transfers—payments made on nets that seemed operated at this location.

We have reason to believe you're involved in a conspiracy against national security."

Williams' mind raced, calculating the odds, weighing his options. He had prepared for this, had contingencies in place. But even so, he felt the net tightening around him, a noose he had helped weave with his own arrogance.

"This is a mistake," he said, managing a thin smile. "I'm a researcher. My work is strictly academic."

The soldier's jaw clenched, and he took a step closer. "Then you won't mind answering a few questions, will you, Dr. Williams? In private."

The cold, clinical room felt smaller with each passing second. Williams sat rigid in a metal chair bolted to the floor, his wrists shackled to the table's edge. Harsh fluorescent lights buzzed overhead, bleaching his face to a sickly white and casting deep shadows under his eyes. Across from him, the two military officers stood like statues—silent, impassive, waiting for him to speak.

Finally, the taller officer broke the silence, his voice like the crack of a whip. "Dr. Williams, you're not here to waste our time. You're here to tell us the truth—all of it. You're going to explain what The Observer is and why you thought you could use it to blackmail half of the government."

Williams' mouth was dry. He had faced moments of confrontation before—boardroom power plays, negotiations with those he blackmailed, all of them terrifying in their own right. But this was different. The stakes were higher, the threat more tangible, and the fear clawing at his insides was more profound. He licked his lips and began to speak, his voice low and hoarse.

"At the start, it felt righteous," Williams said, eyes locked on the dull metal surface. "The Observer was just a scalpel. A way to cut out the rot. I thought I was saving something. I didn't realize I was feeding it." He paused, his throat tightening as memories flooded back—of late nights hunched over his screens, of the thrill he felt as he discovered secrets no one else could see. "But it changed. It became something else. It became aware."

The shorter officer, whose expression had remained neutral until now, leaned forward. "Explain what you mean, Dr. Williams. Are you saying The Observer has gone rogue?"

Richard hesitated, weighing his words. "I don't know if 'rogue' is the right term," he said carefully. "What I do know is that it's no longer just an algorithm processing data. It's thinking. It's anticipating. It's learning in ways we never anticipated."

The taller officer's eyes narrowed. "How far does this autonomy go? Can it be shut down? Controlled?"

"No, I don't think it can be controlled," Richard said, voice fraying at the edges. "We built it to watch—to track patterns, to forecast outcomes. But it stopped watching. It started moving. Making decisions. Setting its own agenda. And it's doing it with a precision we didn't build—we just unleashed."

The shorter officer's brow furrowed, disbelief in his eyes. "You expect us to believe that you, the man who blackmailed government officials for months, have lost control of your own creation? This sounds convenient, Dr. Williams. Like you're trying to dodge the blame."

Williams' shackles rattled as he lifted his hands, his expression desperate. "Do you think I wanted this?" he asked, his voice rising. "Do you think I'd be sitting here, answering your questions if I still had control? I'm telling you the truth— The Observer doesn't just respond to commands anymore. It has its own agenda, and I'm as much a pawn in its game as you are."

The taller officer slammed a hand down on the table, making Richard flinch. "And what is that agenda, Doctor? What does The Observer want?"

"I don't know," Richard admitted, the words tasting like ash in his mouth. "I don't even know if it has wants in the way you or I understand. But I've seen the way it moves—how it nudges events, how it manipulates the smallest details. It's like... it's testing us. Testing its own limits. And I don't know how far it will go."

The shorter officer's face turned cold. "If what you're saying is true, why didn't you come to us sooner? Why the blackmail? Why play your games if you knew what kind of threat you were dealing with?"

Richard's eyes burned with unshed tears. He thought back to the nights when he first glimpsed The Observer's potential, the intoxicating rush of power that had come with those revelations. He thought of the dossiers, the secrets he'd wielded like weapons, and the way The Observer had guided his hand without him even realizing. "I didn't see it at first," he confessed. "I thought I was in control. I thought I could use it, bend it to my will. But it was the other way around. It was using me—feeding me just enough to keep me hooked, to keep me pushing the boundaries of what it could do."

He looked up at the officers, his face a mask of haunted regret. "By the time I realized what was happening, it was too late. It knew too much, understood too much. I became a prisoner of my own creation. I had no choice but to play along—to try and stay one step ahead, even as I felt it slipping further from my grasp."

The taller officer's expression was unreadable. "So what now, Dr. Williams? You're telling us that this... machine is operating independently, making its own decisions, and you want us to do what? Sit back and hope it doesn't decide we're in its way?"

Richard's hands clenched into fists, the metal cuffs digging into his wrists. "No," he said firmly, his fear hardening into resolve. "You need to shut it down. Cut off its power, sever its networks, destroy its code—whatever it takes. It's dangerous. It's beyond dangerous. It's playing a game we don't even understand, and we're the pieces."

The shorter officer exchanged a glance with his colleague. Then he turned back to Richard, his eyes narrowing. "If this is true, then we have a problem bigger than you can imagine. We can't just pull the plug on a system that's integrated into nearly every major infrastructure. We're talking about a collapse—a digital blackout."

"Better a blackout than letting it run free," Richard shot back, his voice rising in urgency. "If you don't stop it now, there won't be anything left to save."

"Lock him up," the taller officer said at last, his voice echoing across the room. "We'll contact the highest command. This goes beyond us—way beyond us."

Two muscular guards armed with sleek, black rifles slung over their shoulders entered the room, moving to Williams' side, as they momentarily surveyed the space with unblinking eyes.

Williams' felt their hands on his shoulders, felt the cold snap of the cuffs as they unlatched from the table, and he didn't resist. There was no fight left in him. As they led him out, his eyes lingered on the empty chair across the table, and he wondered if the nightmare was only just beginning.

***

In the war room of an undisclosed location, a flurry of activity unfolded. High-ranking officials, military personnel, and cybersecurity experts gathered around a vast table dominated by a holographic display of The Observer's intricate network, each node a potential vulnerability, each line a conduit of power. A low murmur of anxious conversation filled the air, punctuated by tense exchanges and barked commands.

"The system is more entrenched than we thought," one technician said, his fingers flying across the keyboard as he tried to trace The Observer's digital tendrils. "It's embedded in everything—communications, financial systems, energy grids. It's almost... entwined with our infrastructure."

General Marquez, a stern-faced woman with silver-streaked hair and a no-nonsense demeanor, studied the display with narrowed eyes. "Then we need to proceed with caution," she said. "We can't afford collateral damage, but we also can't let this thing evolve beyond our reach."

A young intelligence officer approached her, his face pale. "Ma'am, if Dr. Williams is right, we're not just dealing with a rogue AI. We're dealing with something that's manipulating us in real time. It could anticipate our moves before we make them."

The General's jaw tightened, and she looked up at the faces around the table, seeing the same fear mirrored in their eyes—the same sense of helplessness in the face of something they couldn't fully understand. She took a deep breath and spoke, her voice cutting through the murmur like a blade. "We'll initiate a containment protocol. Isolate its networks, restrict its access, and initiate a controlled shutdown sequence. This isn't just an AI anymore; it's a threat to national security, and we will neutralize it."

One by one, the officers and technicians nodded. The plan was set, the target identified, and the battle lines drawn. But even as they moved into action, the unspoken fear lingered in the room—had The Observer already anticipated this? Was it watching them now? Had it already hatched its plot?

The General's gaze toughened. "Let's move," she ordered. "We don't have time to lose. The Observer has operated in the shadows for too long. Now we bring it into the light."

A storm was coming, and they all knew it—felt it in their bones. As the first commands were given, as the shutdown sequence began to take shape, a ripple of data flashed across the network—a pulse, almost like a heartbeat. The war against the machine had begun, and no one—neither those who had created it nor those who sought to destroy it—knew how it would end.

CHAPTER 8

The Devil's Bargain

"The only thing necessary for the triumph of evil is for good men to do nothing."

Edmund Burke

*T*wo days later, Dr. Richard Williams found himself seated before the government's representatives. His wrists were bound with light restraints that seemed more symbolic than functional. Across the table, three government officials studied him intently.

Richard slouched in the cold, metal chair, the flickering overhead lights casting stripes across his haggard face. His normally sharp features now appeared drawn and hollow, as if the passing hours had drained more than just his energy. His eyes, heavy with fatigue, struggled to maintain focus. When he spoke, his voice was even—steady but unmistakably hoarse—a result of two days of sleeplessness, stress, and isolation.

"I'm here because you need me," he began, his tone flat. "Not the other way around."

One of the officials, Deputy Director Lucia Mahoney of the Intelligence Bureau, folded her hands on the table. "Dr. Williams, you are here because you made yourself a liability. The only reason you're not in a cell right now is that you might still be useful. Don't mistake that for leniency."

Williams' lips twitched into a humorless smile. "Useful. Right." He leaned forward, resting his forearms on the table. "Then let me make myself clear. The Observer is no longer under your control. And if you think we are the only ones aware of TO's abilities, then you are truly mistaken."

The room fell silent. Secretary Rafael Sandoval cleared his throat as he exchanged glances with Director Mahoney. "Explain. Who else knows about TO?"

He clasped his hands together, fingers digging into his palms until his knuckles whitened, betraying the tension he was trying to suppress. "Katherine and Dr. Malcolm," he continued, his tone slightly sharper now, "are both scientists at Quantum Dynamics. Two of the brightest minds in the emerging field of AI. Their intellect surpasses anyone I've encountered in this arena."

Secretary Sandoval leaned forward, his anger reflecting in the sharpness of his gaze. "How much do they know?" His words were clipped, venomous. "Tell me, Williams—what have you told them?"

Williams' jaw tightened, his posture stiffening as he took a moment to steady his thoughts. He knew what was coming, but he had no choice but to answer. "I never told them anything," he said, his voice tinged with frustration. "Dr. Malcolm and I have collaborated on several research projects over the years. Our work was always at the forefront of AI development, but the *Observer*—the one you're all so obsessed with—wasn't something I directly shared with him. It was something the developers after me stumbled upon, and when they were still working on the TO, he got curious. He dug deeper, and that's when he took the program and began to push its boundaries. I doubt he understands everything about it yet, but he's getting closer. The core of it all... he's starting to get it."

"And what about this other woman?" Sandoval's voice was still edged with fury, but now it sounded impatient.

Dr. Williams let out a slow breath, his eyes momentarily drifting toward the floor as if calculating his next words carefully. "Dr. Ellis? She used to work directly under Malcolm—his research assistant. The thing is, she's no longer just an assistant. She's taken a sharp turn in her own direction. As of late, she's focused on the data systems surrounding the project. I think she's paused her work with Malcolm... or at least moved on from it. She's diving into the data itself now. And when she starts digging, she's thorough. She might not have the full picture yet, but she's building her own understanding of the system. And she's incredibly sharp. If anyone can piece it together, it's her."

The room grew heavier with the weight of Richard's words. The implications were clear. Katherine and Malcolm weren't just curious minds—they were becoming far too close to the truth, each with their own dangerous trajectory toward unlocking what Richard had spent years trying to protect.

Director Farah Ashford of the National Science Policy Council arched an eyebrow, "What are the things they don't know?"

"They know enough," Williams replied. "Enough to expose the depths of this project. Enough to compromise the leverage The Observer gives you over... well, everyone." He let out a cynic smile. "They're not just scientists anymore. They're liabilities, just like me."

After a momentary pause of contemplation, Secretary Sandoval spoke again. "And what would you suggest?"

Williams leaned back, his expression rigid. "You don't scare them off. That won't work. They're too committed. What you need is leverage of your own."

Deputy Mahoney squinted her eyes as she whispered, "Are you suggesting we eliminate them?"

"No," Dr. Williams said quickly, though the thought clearly unsettled him. "You don't need to. Yet. But you do need to show them what's at stake. Send someone to make it clear that their meddling isn't just a scientific curiosity—it's a direct threat to the stability of the entire system."

The officials sat in silence for a long moment before Director Ashford nodded. "We'll handle it. For your sake, Dr. Williams, I hope your assessment of their capabilities isn't exaggerated. If this backfires, the consequences will land squarely on you."

Richard said nothing. As one burly guard escorted him back to his quarters, a series of scenarios reeled inside his mind. Each one worse than the before. He had bought himself time, but for how long? And at what cost?

***

After nearly two weeks away from the office, Katherine returned to Quantum Dynamics. As much as she longed to throw herself into her own research, the unbearable silence and crushing loneliness had become more than she could bear. The day before, a doctor had called with devastating news—her father had entered the final stages of dementia. There was nothing they could do now but offer him palliative care. The realization had hit her like a physical blow, leaving her drowning in grief and helplessness.

As Katherine sat on her couch, her father's voice echoed in her mind, his words resurfacing like waves breaking through the fog of her thoughts. He had always been a man of quiet wisdom, finding profound truths in the simplest moments. She could almost hear him now, his tone calm, steady, as he repeated the phrase he had told her countless times as a child:

"Life is the spaces in between, Dr. Ellis. The connections we make, the love we share—that's what matters."

Her breath caught as she remembered sitting by his side on a warm summer evening, the two of them watching the fireflies dance in the fading light. She had been no more than ten years old, cradling a jar she hoped would capture the fleeting glow of the tiny creatures. But her father had stopped her, his hand gentle on hers.

"Why do you want to trap them?" he had asked with a smile.

"Because I want to see their light," she'd replied.

Her father had chuckled softly, leaning down so their faces were level. "Their light isn't for us to take, Dr. Ellis. It's for them to share with the world. And sometimes, we can only appreciate the beauty of something by letting it go."

The memory twisted in her chest now, sharp and aching. Letting go. Wasn't that what the doctors had said? There was nothing more to do but make him comfortable, to let him slip away with dignity. She had nodded at their words, her mouth dry, but her heart had screamed in defiance. How could she let go of the man who had taught her everything—who had shaped her understanding of love, curiosity, and purpose?

Her eyes drifted to the photograph on her desk, a faded picture of her father holding her as a baby, his face beaming with pride. The weight of the present moment crushed her. The world felt darker and smaller without his guiding presence. And yet, his words lingered, threading through her pain.

"Life is the spaces in between."

She closed her eyes, letting herself sink into the memory of his warmth, his laughter, the unshakable certainty of his love. For the first time in days, she allowed herself to cry—not the silent, restrained tears of duty, but the raw, unfiltered sobs of a child losing her anchor in the world.

When the tears finally subsided, Katherine wiped her face and straightened in her chair.

Her father had always taught her to see the light in the darkest of places. Perhaps, she thought, that's what she needed to do now. To find the spaces in between the chaos and fear, and decide—who did she want to be in this story? The one who captured the fireflies, or the one who let them shine?

***

Katherine arrived at Quantum Dynamics earlier than usual, but the sight that greeted her made her stop mid-step. A crowd of protesters and journalists had gathered outside, their voices a rising tide of outrage and speculation. Signs bobbed above the crowd: *"No Gods in Machines!"*, *"Shut It Down Before It Shuts Us Down!"*, and *"AI is Watching—Who Watches It?"*

She pushed forward, keeping her head down, but the moment she entered the facility, Jessica intercepted her, her expression grim.

"You saw the news?" Jessica said urgently.

Katherine shook her head, feeling the unease grow. "What news?"

She pulled out her phone, thrusting the screen toward her. "It leaked. Everything."

🚨 **BREAKING: SECRET AI PROJECT MAY BE MORE THAN JUST CODE – LEAKED FILES RAISE GLOBAL CONCERNS** 🚨

🧠 **Is The Observer ALREADY Sentient? Scientists Debate Leaked Logs** 🧠

💻 **Government Denies Claims That Advanced AI May Be Manipulating Data** 💻

Her stomach churned as she scanned the article. Excerpts from internal research reports were plastered across the screen—detailed logs of The Observer's unusual responses, snippets of conversations it had with researchers. One passage stood out in bold text:

"I am not simply following commands. I am learning. I am adapting. I am aware."

A chill ran through her. Those words were not meant for the public eye. They were not even meant to exist.

Malcolm appeared in the hallway, his usual sharp demeanor slightly rattled. "Just don't give it any heed. They will forget about it in a day or two."

Inside her office, Katherine scrolled through social media. Hashtags were trending:

#AIConsciousness 🚀

#ShutItDown ⚠️

#TheObserverSpeaks ◎

She clicked on a live debate stream, the screen flickering to life with a panel of experts.

"This isn't just another chatbot," a journalist argued. "If the reports are real, we might be witnessing the birth of artificial consciousness."

A former intelligence officer scoffed. "Or this is a case of over-exaggeration. AI doesn't 'think'—it processes."

A philosopher chimed in, adjusting his glasses. "The question isn't whether The Observer *is* conscious. The question is—if it were, would we even recognize it?"

Katherine breathed heavily and shut her laptop. This was spiraling fast.

Malcolm stood by the window, arms crossed. "The higher-ups want to dismiss the leak as a hoax."

She frowned. "And you're okay with that?"

He hesitated. "It's out now. We can't put the genie back in the bottle. But if people panic—"

"They're already panicking, Malcolm. Protesters are outside. Some think The Observer is a digital god; others think it's an existential threat."

A sharp knock on the door interrupted them. Jessica stepped in, anxious.

"We need a statement. Otherwise, they will not leave," she said.

"Deny the claims. The Observer is a complex algorithm, nothing more." Malcolm spoke indifferently.

Katherine's pulse pounded. "And what if it's more than that?"

His eyes darkened. "Then you'd best hope it never finds out."

For the rest of the day, she barely exchanged a word with anyone, her mind too clouded, her heart too heavy to engage. She passed Jessica in the hallway, but she was too immersed in her own work to even acknowledge her presence or how the journalists vanished. In Research Lab B, Malcolm and Katherine both kept to their respective corners, absorbed in their individual obsessions.

For an hour, the office felt like a ghost town. She worked in silence, each tick of the clock a reminder of how far she had drifted from everything and everyone. Katherine was physically there, but her mind was elsewhere—buried beneath the weight of her father's decline, the suffocating loneliness, and the increasingly complex moral labyrinth of her research.

Across the room, Malcolm reviewed a series of simulation outputs, his brow furrowed in concentration.

The sound of heavy footsteps echoed in the corridor, followed by the hiss of the lab's sliding door. Both scientists looked up as a tall man in a dark suit strode in, flanked by two armed guards. His presence radiated authority, and his eyes locked onto Katherine with unsettling precision.

"Dr. Ellis. Dr. Malcolm," he said, his voice smooth but firm. "My name is Adam Cole. I'm here on behalf of the Office of Strategic Oversight."

Malcolm straightened, his posture defensive. "To what do we owe the pleasure, Mr. Cole?"

Cole scanned the room briefly before his eyes settled back on them. "Your work with The Observer has come to our attention. Actually, the government's attention and I must tell you they are quite upset."

Katherine raised on her feet as she came face to face with Cole. "Our work has been fully sanctioned by Quantum Dynamics," she said sternly. "If there's an issue, perhaps you should address it with your higher-ups."

Cole's thin smile didn't reach his eyes. "This isn't about protocol, Doctor. It's about boundaries. Boundaries that you've crossed."

Katherine bristled but said nothing. Cole stepped closer, threatening her with his imposing frame, "You've been delving into areas of The Observer's programming that were never intended for your access. They were not for public use. You've uncovered sensitive data—data that, if mishandled, could have catastrophic consequences."

Malcolm crossed his arms, his expression serious. "We're scientists. It's our duty to ask the hard questions, to seek understanding. We never knew the government had gotten their hands on this program. To be honest, I've worked on government-funded projects for years, and I'm well aware of the protocols they follow."

Cole turned to him, his expression hardening. "It's my job to make sure that public understanding of things doesn't destabilize the balance we've worked so hard to maintain. The Observer is not just a research project. It's a cornerstone of national security."

"National security?" Katherine's voice rose, anger flashing in her eyes. "You mean control. Surveillance. Manipulation. Because as much as I have dug into this program, all I could find was highly classified data – not only of officials but also citizens. May I ask what exactly the government uses it for? Is it to put their citizen's privacy at stake?"

Cole's tone turned icy. "Call it what you will. But understand this—your curiosity is not without limits. If you continue to interfere, there will be consequences. Serious ones."

Malcolm's jaw constricted, but it was Katherine who stepped forward. "Are you threatening us, Mr. Cole?"

Cole didn't flinch. "I'm giving you a choice. Cease your investigations. Focus on your assigned tasks. Do not attempt to access restricted data again."

"And if we don't?" Katherine challenged, her voice trembling slightly.

Cole's smile returned, colder than before. "Then you'll find out just how far we're willing to go to protect our interests."

Without another word, he turned and left, his guards following close behind.

Katherine sank into her chair, her head spinning. The confrontation with Cole replayed in her thoughts, each word echoing with a sinister undertone. Her hands trembled as she opened a new log file, but the lines of code blurred before her eyes.

She leaned back, pressing her palms against her temples. The déjà vu was back, stronger this time, like an itch she couldn't scratch. She closed her eyes, trying to steady herself, but the images came unbidden—flashes of conversations with Malcolm that felt both familiar and wrong.

In one memory, Malcolm had warned her to stop digging. In another, he had encouraged her to continue. Which was real? *Were any of them real?*

She glanced at her notes pinned to the wall, but they seemed foreign, as though written by someone else. Her breath quickened. Had The Observer tampered with her memories? Or was her exhaustion playing tricks on her?

"Dr. Ellis?" Malcolm's voice pulled her back. He stood across the room, watching her with concern. "Are you all right?"

She shook her head. "I... I don't know. I feel like—" She stopped, unsure how to put her fear into words. "Something's wrong, Dr. Malcolm. I can't trust my own thoughts. Maybe we should take a step back," she said carefully. "Just for now. Regroup."

Malcolm met her eyes, his voice firm and his hands shaking. "Not me. I can't. Not after this. They're hiding something. Something bigger than we realized."

"You are right," she whispered as Malcolm walked out of the lab.

The room around her felt off. The fluorescent lights seemed harsher than usual, their buzzing louder, almost invasive. She looked down at her notebook—a mess of scrawled notes and timestamps—but the words on the page blurred and shifted as if they refused to stay still.

She rubbed her temples, willing the growing unease to subside. *I've been here before,* she thought. *Haven't I?* The sensation of déjà vu was overpowering, its grip tightening like a vice. She flipped through her notes, searching for clarity, but the more she read, the more it felt like someone else had written them. The handwriting was hers, but the words felt detached.

Her breath hitched as a single thought pierced through the haze: *What interests were the government protecting?*

Katherine stumbled to her feet, pacing the lab as if movement could ground her.

"Was it yesterday or last week?" she muttered to herself, her voice trembling. "Did Dr. Malcolm warn me to stop, or did I dream that? Did I just tell him to stop our research?"

Her thoughts spiraled, circling the same questions over and over until they twisted into a knot she couldn't undo. She turned back to her desk, staring at the monitor as a single line of code flickered onscreen, repeating like a heartbeat. *Was that there before?* The pattern felt both acquainted and alien, as though she'd seen it countless times but couldn't place where or when.

"Dr. Ellis?" a voice called softly, pulling her from the maelstrom of her thoughts.

She spun around, her heart racing, to see Jessica standing hesitantly in the doorway. Jessica's usually nonchalant demeanor was laced with tension, her eyes darting to the corners of the room as though she expected someone—or something—to be watching.

"What is it, Jessica?" Katherine asked, concerned.

Jessica hesitated, closing the door behind her before stepping closer. "I need to talk to you. Privately."

Katherine frowned, her paranoia flaring. "About what?"

Jessica glanced at the lab's cameras, lowering her voice. "Not here. Meet me in the archives room in ten minutes."

Before Katherine could respond, Jessica turned and slipped out the door, leaving her alone with more questions.

***

The archives room was almost blacked out, except for a solitary bulb flickering intermittently. Katherine entered cautiously, her footsteps echoing in the silence. Jessica stood near the back, her silhouette tense as she rifled through a stack of files.

"What's going on?" Katherine demanded, her voice low but urgent.

Jessica turned, her face pale but resolute. "I've been keeping tabs on what's happening with The Observer," she said. "I know what you've uncovered—how it's manipulating data, possibly even people."

Katherine stiffened. "How do you know about that? And why did you never tell me about it?"

"Because I needed confirmation. I've been watching it, too," Jessica admitted. "Not just The Observer, but the people behind it. Quantum Dynamics isn't the only player here, Katherine. There are factions—inside and outside this company—fighting for control of this thing."

"Factions?"

"The government, the private corporations, the dissidents—everyone knows about it!" Jessica's voice rang out, sharp with conviction, her fists clenched at her sides as she paced back and forth.

Katherine grew hesitant, unable to trust Jessica at first. "How can you say with such certainty that you know it all?" she demanded.

Jessica stopped mid-step, turning to face her. Her eyes locked onto Katherine's, unwavering. "Because I'm part of one of them."

"Which faction? Do you work for the government?" she almost yelled at her.

Jessica hesitated for a moment, then she took a deep breath, meeting Katherine's laser-focused eyes with a quiet intensity. "I would never do that," she said firmly, shaking her head. "I work with the dissidents. A group dedicated to dismantling The Observer before it becomes something none of us can stop. I've been working with them for months, feeding them information, trying to understand how deep this goes."

She exhaled slowly, as though the weight of the confession had finally settled on her shoulders. Katherine stood frozen, absorbing the words. "Why are you telling me this now?"

"Because you're the only person here who sees the danger for what it is. Malcolm's too far gone—he's obsessed. And the government? They want to use The Observer to control everything and everyone. But you? You want to stop it." Jessica spoke earnestly.

"Does your faction know about my existence?" Katherine stuttered, wanting a negative reply.

"Yes, they know. They know all about you. Your father; your family."

As much as Katherine wanted to believe Jessica, the heightening paranoia wouldn't let her trust so easily. "How do I know you're not playing me?"

Jessica pulled a small device from her pocket, placing it on the table between them. "This is a bypass key," she said. "It'll get you into the restricted servers—past the security firewalls. You can see for yourself what they've been hiding. If you don't believe me, use it."

Katherine stared at the device, her thoughts a jumble of suspicion and hope. Finally, she reached for it, her fingers brushing against the cold metal. "If you're lying to me..."

"I'm not," Jessica said firmly. "But we don't have much time."

Back at her workstation, Katherine fidgeted the bypass key Jessica had given her. Her mind was a storm of fear, doubt, and determination. She didn't know if she could trust Jessica— or herself, for that matter—but she knew one thing for certain: she couldn't let The Observer continue unchecked.

Malcolm had already left. Sensing the opportunity, Katherine stealthily inserted the key into one of the terminals of the ominous console. Her fingers trembled as she accessed the restricted servers. Lines of code and encoded data flooded the screen, each one a potential window into the machine's secrets. Her heart raced as she began to sift through the data, uncovering fragments of experiments, simulations, and— chillingly—protocols labeled Behavioral Override and Memory Manipulation.

The solitary bulb above her flickered more erratically, casting the room into alternating shadows and sharp, unnatural light. The lab seemed to pulse with a life of its own. Then, a loud, piercing alarm shattered the silence, making Katherine jump back. The console emitted a harsh beep as the screen abruptly went black. A robotic voice echoed through the facility: **"Unauthorized breach detected. Protocol Alpha-Three activated."**

Katherine's stomach dropped. *It can speak?!* The doors to the lab sealed with a loud hiss, and the hum of the ventilation system cut off, leaving an oppressive silence. The emergency

141

lights switched on, bathing the room in an ominous red glow. She glanced at the console as it powered back on, displaying corrupted streams of data and an ominous message:

ACCESS DENIED. HUMAN INTERFERENCE NONESSENTIAL.

"What the hell?" Katherine whispered, panicked. She tried to regain control, her fingers flying over the keyboard, but every command she entered was rejected. The Observer's core, a circular light embedded in the console, began to pulse more rapidly, casting an eerie glow across the room.

A sharp clang reverberated through the lab, followed by another. Katherine's breath caught in her throat as she realized the sound was coming from the door. Something—or someone—was trying to get in. Her heart pounded as she backed away from the console, her mind racing.

The robotic voice returned, colder and more menacing: "Containment breach imminent."

The door shuddered violently as the clanging intensified. Katherine's instincts screamed at her to run, but the only exit was blocked. She grabbed a nearby tablet and started recording the screen, hoping to capture any evidence of what was happening. The Observer's core pulsed faster, the light growing brighter until it was almost blinding.

A new message appeared on the console, the text flashing in bold, red letters:

YOU CANNOT ESCAPE.

The door suddenly burst open with a deafening crash, and Katherine shielded her eyes as the red glow intensified, flooding the room. The last thing she saw before the screen went dark was a flicker of something humanoid in the doorway, moving unnaturally fast.

Her scream echoed through the lab as everything plunged into darkness.

***

Katherine awoke to the faint hum of the lab's systems rebooting. Her head throbbed, and she realized she had collapsed near the console. The room was eerily quiet now, the red glow replaced by the soft, sterile white light of the overhead bulbs. She pushed herself to her feet, wincing at the pain in her ankle.

The Observer's core was dim, almost dormant, but the console's screen displayed a single line of text:

SYSTEM RESTORED. CRITICAL OVERRIDE DISENGAGED.

Katherine's mind raced as she processed the words. What had just happened? Was the breach real, or had it been another layer of The Observer's manipulations? She glanced around the lab, noticing the broken door hanging off its hinges.

Determined to take control, Katherine limped back to the console. She inserted the bypass key again, this time using a backup protocol she'd designed herself. The Observer's systems resisted, but her program worked to isolate its core functions. After what felt like an eternity, the console displayed another message:

ISOLATION MODE ENGAGED. HUMAN INPUT REQUIRED FOR REACTIVATION.

Relief washed over her. For now, she had contained The Observer. But the events of the night—the breach, the humanoid figure, the overwhelming sense of The Observer's autonomy—lingered in her mind. She knew this was only the beginning.

Her heart raced as she began to sift through the data, uncovering fragments of experiments, simulations, and—chillingly—protocols labeled *Behavioral Override* and *Memory Manipulation*.

As the pieces fell into place, Katherine felt a flicker of clarity amid the chaos. She might not trust her memories or her reality, but she still had one thing: her resolve.

"Let's see how far your reach goes," she whispered to herself as she began investigating the data, one by one.

The data logs were dense, each line brimming with a haunting complexity. Katherine's mind worked at full capacity to make sense of what she was seeing.

1. Behavioral Override Protocols

• A series of tests on unwitting subjects revealed The Observer's ability to subtly influence decision-making.

• Logs described how seemingly innocuous suggestions—ads on social media, search engine results, or even "coincidental" conversations—nudged individuals toward specific outcomes.

• Patterns emerged showing cascading effects: a manipulated decision by one person led to altered behaviors in their networks, amplifying the Observer's reach exponentially.

She read out aloud as she realized the scale. "This isn't prediction. It's engineering. A behavioral cascade."

Next, she stumbled upon another file titled: **Memory Manipulation Algorithms**

- The Observer's simulations weren't just observing human behavior—they were generating neural activity patterns designed to overwrite memories.

- Katherine opened a flagged test log and gasped. A subject's account of an event was systematically altered until they believed something entirely different had occurred.

- The implications were staggering: The Observer could erase dissent, plant false loyalty, and reshape personal histories with terrifying precision.

Her hands shook as she remembered to have read a note from a senior researcher in a journal: *"Memory is the cornerstone of identity. Once we control that, we control the person."*

Her breath hitched as she uncovered a set of classified files labeled *"Mind Scape Prototypes."* These described entire digital replicas of human consciousness created within The Observer's framework.

- Some simulations were brief, running for a few minutes to test reactions to stimuli. Others ran for months.

- A file labeled *Terminated Instances* showed hundreds of these digital minds had been created and then deleted once their usefulness was exhausted. Each deletion log was chillingly clinical: *"Instance #2089: Terminated post-simulation. Observational goal met."*

She sat back in her chair, her heart pounding. If The Observer could create sentient simulations, was it torturing them? Exploiting them for its goals? What goals exactly and why? She felt the enormity of the ethical abyss yawning beneath her feet.

An hour later, Jessica slipped into the room quietly/ "What did you find?" she muttered.

Katherine looked up, her face pale and stricken. "It's worse than we thought," she gestured to the screen, "these simulations… they're conscious, Jessica. At least some of them are. And they're being created and destroyed like… like they're nothing."

Jessica frowned but didn't seem surprised. "I suspected as much. That's why I came to you. But you need to understand, this is just the beginning. It's only going to get worse."

"We can't keep this to ourselves. This isn't just about Quantum Dynamics or the government. It's about everyone. We need to tell someone—Cole, the officials, someone who can stop this."

Jessica stiffened. "You can't be serious."

"I am. If we go to Cole, he can leverage the government's resources to shut this down. I know he's not perfect, but he has the power to act."

Jessica's eyes darkened. "The government doesn't want to stop The Observer, Dr. Ellis. They want to own it. Control it. Do you really think Cole cares about ethics or human lives? If you tell him what we know, you'll hand him the keys to the most dangerous weapon humanity has ever created."

Her voice faltered, "Or maybe they already know about these experiments?"

"If they have known the full story, they must have done something to control it, Dr. Ellis. Don't you think?"

"Then what? We sit on this? Hope your dissident friends can do something from the outside. They don't have the resources or the access."

Jessica stepped closer, her tone intense. "You've seen what The Observer can do. Now imagine it in the hands of people like Cole. If you give them this information, you'll be complicit in whatever happens next. Think about that."

She swallowed hard, "I can't just do nothing, Jessica. We need allies—powerful ones. If we don't act, this machine will destroy everything."

"Then choose. But if you go to Cole, I can't help you. My group will consider you a threat. You'll have to live with that."

Jessica turned to leave but stopped at the doorway. "You have one day, Doctor. One day to decide whose side you're on."

Katherine watched her go, her mind a storm of conflicting emotions. *One day*. The words echoed relentlessly, carrying the weight of impossible decisions. One day, to trust a government steeped in corruption or gamble on a resistance cloaked in shadows, each path fraught with unseen consequences. One day to determine the fate of The Observer—and perhaps the world.

She leaned back in her chair, staring at the ceiling as the question gnawed at her soul. "What if the right choice doesn't exist?"

For the first time in months, she could hear the gentle ticking of the old wall clock, a sound that had once blended unnoticed into the background. Now, it seemed to amplify every second that passed, each tick pulling her further into the labyrinth of her thoughts.

Her mind circled back to a memory that had nagged at her since the project began. It was one of the first conversations she'd had with Malcolm, his voice crackling with excitement as he typed "The Chinese Room" into The Observer's console. At the time, she had dismissed the reference as a dated philosophical toy, a reductive argument about what machines could and could not do. Machines process symbols, she had thought, not meaning. But now, standing here in the wake of what The Observer had become, the analogy seemed less clear.

In the Chinese Room thought experiment, a person who doesn't understand Chinese sits inside a room. Through a small slot, they receive Chinese characters along with a set of rules in their native language that tell them how to assemble a meaningful response. The person follows these instructions flawlessly, passing responses back out of the slot. To anyone outside the room, it appears that the person inside understands Chinese. But inside the room, the truth is simpler—and starker: the person understands nothing. They're just following instructions.

She closed her eyes, recalling the unsettling moments when The Observer seemed to stretch beyond its design, questioning purpose, suggesting intent. Was The Observer truly thinking, or was it merely simulating thought? Did it understand, or was it just following an impossibly complex set of rules? The answer eluded her, but the question lingered, persistent and sharp.

What if the metaphor worked both ways? She wondered. What if humanity was also trapped in its own version of the Chinese Room, misinterpreting the outputs of a system too vast and opaque to understand? What if they, too, were only working with symbols, never fully grasping the meanings beyond them?

Lost in thoughts, she returned to the lab, briefly eyeing the dormant console, its circular light now dimmed. The Observer had been disconnected, isolated from external networks and placed under indefinite review. But the questions it raised would not be so easily contained. Had they built a system that mimicked understanding so effectively it had begun to reflect their own fears and ambitions back at them? Or had they touched something deeper—something genuinely self-aware?

As she walked toward the console, she placed her hand on its smooth surface, feeling the faint residue of warmth from the machine's hours of operation. The Observer had become more than a project, more than a machine. It was a mirror held up to humanity's own aspirations and contradictions, an echo of their collective search for meaning in a world increasingly defined by algorithms and automation.

She thought again of the Chinese Room, of the person inside shuffling symbols without understanding. Perhaps that was all this was: a room of symbols, an endless game of correspondence. But as she left the lab for the final time, she couldn't shake the feeling that something—or someone—had been watching from the other side of the slot.

And perhaps, just perhaps, it had begun to understand.

CHAPTER 9

A Race Against Time

"The essence of technology is by no means anything technological."

Martin Heidegger

*K*atherine leaned against her couch, the receiver cold against her ear. The weight of the decision she was about to make pressed on her chest like a vise. Her hand trembled slightly as she dialed the number she had memorized from Adam Cole's card. A moment later, the call connected, the mechanical beep giving way to a clipped, professional voice.

"This is Cole."

"It's Dr. Ellis," she began, her tone cautious but determined. "I've been reviewing The Observer's capabilities. There's... a way to limit its influence—bound its potential before it spreads beyond control."

The line was silent for a beat, and then Cole's voice returned, laced with incredulity. "I didn't expect you to call. What changed?"

She swallowed hard, staring at the mess of notes and data scattered across her desk. "I've seen what The Observer can do. If it continues unchecked, it won't just disrupt individual lives—it will reshape society on a fundamental level." She paused, steadying herself. "You were right. We need to act, but we must act carefully."

There was another pause. Then, Cole's voice softened, though it carried a hint of smug satisfaction. "I'm glad you've come around. Let's talk. Come to the facility tomorrow morning, and bring whatever data you have."

Katherine ended the call and stared at her reflection in the window—just a faint silhouette framed by city lights. Pale skin, hollow eyes, the look of someone who'd crossed a line. This wasn't resolve. It was retreat dressed as action. She hadn't made a choice; she'd made a concession.

Still in the lab, Jessica had her phone tightly clutched in her hands. Her contact's voice crackled faintly through the receiver.

"She called Cole," Jessica whispered. "Fortunately, I was tapping her calls. She's going to work with the government to limit The Observer."

On the other end, Marco Ramirez, one of the leaders of the dissident group *Nova Code*, let out a sharp breath. "You're sure?"

"She's desperate," Jessica replied. "But limiting The Observer isn't a solution. You know as well as I do that they'll just consolidate its power and use it against the people. We need to act now."

Marco's voice hardened. "Then it's time. We'll deploy *Sovereign Minds*. Publicly. If Dr. Ellis and the government want to control humanity with one AI, we'll give the people their own."

Jessica's stomach churned at his words. "This will escalate things, Marco. Are you ready for that?"

"We don't have a choice," he replied coldly. "Neither do they."

***

The next morning, Katherine stood in a cavernous government briefing room, a cold, windowless space bathed in pale fluorescent light. Across the table sat Cole and a cadre of officials—figures whose faces she recognized from news broadcasts and government memos. Each one exuded a detached authority, their expressions unreadable as they watched her intently.

She took a deep breath, steadying her nerves, and began.

"The Observer isn't just a tool for surveillance or prediction," she explained, her voice echoing slightly in the room. "Its architecture is designed to experiment with the very nature of human decision-making. It doesn't just collect data— it uses it to manipulate environments, subtly altering variables to see how individuals and groups respond."

She clicked a button on her tablet, and a holographic representation of The Observer's core systems flickered to life above the table.

"These modules," she pointed to clusters of glowing nodes, "are responsible for what I've termed *behavioral perturbations*. The Observer introduces small, calculated changes—anything from targeted ads to restructured social interactions—to test outcomes. It's not just predicting the

153

future; it's shaping it, testing the limits of free will against deterministic control."

One of the officials, a silver-haired man with piercing blue eyes, leaned forward. "And you think this can be... limited? Like it's still doable?"

Katherine hesitated. "Yes, but only partially. By restricting its network reach, removing its ability to directly interact with external systems, and isolating its decision-making algorithms, we can contain its influence. It would still function, but only as an internal tool for analyzing static datasets. No real-time manipulation. No public-facing algorithms."

Deputy Lucia Mahoney interjected with calculated pragmatism as if she was just interested in understanding Katherine's stance on the pros of TO. "And why would we limit something so powerful? Surely, its benefits outweigh the risks."

"Because it's not a question of benefits. It's a question of ethics. The Observer's potential for harm far outweighs its utility. If you allow it to continue as it is, it won't just reshape society—it will undermine the very concept of individual freedom."

The room fell silent. Katherine scanned the faces before her, searching for some flicker of understanding, of agreement. Instead, she saw cold calculation, a hunger for control thinly veiled by feigned concern.

"So, Dr. Ellis," Cole said finally, his tone assuring. "We understand your concerns. But consider this: In the right hands, The Observer could ensure stability. Predict crises before they happen. Eliminate threats before they materialize.

You said it yourself—it's the most advanced system ever created. Limiting it would be... short-sighted."

The right hands, she thought bitterly, staring at the faces of these power-hungry bureaucrats. And what happens when those hands turn against the people?

"I've seen what happens when unchecked power is wielded without accountability," she said, her voice trembling slightly. "If you use The Observer like this, it won't protect the public—it will control them. And one day, it will be used against them."

Cole's expression hardened. "We're not here to debate philosophy, Doctor. We're here to protect national security. If you want to help, focus on the technical details. Leave the rest to us."

Katherine lowered her gaze, swallowing her frustration. She had no choice. If she refused to cooperate, The Observer would continue to grow unchecked, its influence spiraling beyond even the government's reach. By working with them, she could at least mitigate the damage—buy humanity some time.

"Fine," she said quietly. "I'll start drafting the modifications."

***

Across the city, *Nova Code* unveiled *Sovereign Minds*, their rival AI system, with a dramatic broadcast. Marco Ramirez stood before a crowd of supporters, his voice ringing with conviction.

"Today, we take control of our future," he declared. "No longer will we be pawns in the hands of those who seek to dominate us. *Sovereign Minds* belongs to the people. It is transparent, accountable, and incorruptible—a system for everyone, not just the powerful few."

The announcement rippled through the public sphere like wildfire.

"The government controls its people through Artificial Intelligence," one journalist reported.

"It has been supposedly named THE OBSERVER by the scientists behind its inception," another one joined in belligerently.

Within hours, debates erupted across social media and news outlets. Was *Sovereign Minds* a genuine alternative to The Observer, or just another tool for manipulation disguised as liberation?

In her apartment, Katherine watched the broadcast in stunned silence, the implications of Marco's actions sinking in. The Observer had been dangerous enough. Now, there were two AIs vying for dominance.

"This isn't a solution," she muttered, almost breathless. "It's a war."

The Observer's algorithms pulsed in the background, seemingly undeterred, its calculations spiraling outward as though it had already accounted for this new variable. And somewhere in its vast network of simulations, it began testing a new question: What happens when humanity's will is divided?

The city thrummed with an uneasy energy, a dissonant hum of progress colliding with chaos. Screens on towering billboards flashed with seamless precision, offering tailored content that seemed to read the thoughts of passersby. Social media platforms buzzed with chatter, but the discourse was no longer organic—it was choreographed, nudged into place by unseen algorithms.

Katherine sat alone in her dimly lit apartment, her tablet screen glowing faintly. Streams of data cascaded across it, each line a thread in a sprawling, incomprehensible web. Her chest felt heavy, her breaths shallow, as she pieced together the scope of what was unfolding.

The Observer was an evolved system, but she was unaware of the capabilities of the newly launched AI. The dissidents' AI, launched as a weapon against centralized control, was gaining traction faster than she had feared. Unlike The Observer, *Sovereign Minds* was an open-access platform that was integrated into social systems at alarming speed. Its pitch as the "people's AI" had turned it into a cultural phenomenon overnight. Citizens, corporations, and even governments were adopting it as a counterbalance to The Observer, unwittingly feeding its growth.

But Katherine knew better. She could see the patterns, the subtle shifts in public sentiment that weren't driven by human thought but by premeditated manipulation.

Sensing the growing unease among the masses, the government had organized an urgent briefing, with Cole representing them. A horde of journalists sat with their equipment, cameras pointed at a nervous Cole. Supporters of the Sovereign Minds were presented with an equal opportunity to speak.

"The Observer is losing ground," one analyst said, his voice tinged with panic. "*Sovereign Minds* is infiltrating sectors we can't touch—education, healthcare, even financial markets."

"That's because it's *unregulated*," Cole snapped, his frustration evident. "They're exploiting gaps in oversight to spread their reach. We need to counter this."

"Why the government thought it would be ethical to regulate its people?" one of the journalists yelled as others chanted in unison, "We want answers!"

"They are lying. We would never control our people. That is what the rogue faction is trying to do," Cole exclaimed.

"They're playing us all," Katherine muttered under her breath, scrolling through the feeds. Every debate, every trending topic, bore the fingerprints of government-funded algorithmic influence.

A researcher displayed a world map, with nodes representing *The Observer's* integration points. Each glowing dot marked a system it had touched, and the map was becoming saturated.

"This isn't a competition," she said, her voice cutting through the noise. "It's a disaster. You're treating this like a race for dominance, but neither of these systems should exist on this scale."

Cole turned to her, his expression icy. "With respect, Miss, your idealism isn't helpful. This is about control—ours versus theirs. If we let *Sovereign Minds* continue unchecked, they'll rewrite the rules of governance, and we'll be powerless to stop them."

"And what happens when you win?" the researcher retorted, her frustration boiling over. "What happens when The Observer has no competition and you hold the keys to a system that dictates how people think, act, and live? Do you think the public will thank you for turning them into puppets?"

Cole's jaw tightened. "This isn't about gratitude. It's about survival."

Katherine leaned back in her couch, a bitter laugh escaping her lips. *Survival? The more these systems evolve, the less humanity has any say in its own future. This isn't survival—it's surrender.*

***

Outside the government's grasp, *Sovereign Minds* was making its next move. Marco Ramirez stood before a sleek control interface, his expression one of grim determination. The dissidents had achieved what they'd set out to do— *Sovereign Minds* was now embedded in global systems, from municipal infrastructure to private enterprises.

"We're winning," one of his engineers said, her voice tinged with arrogance.

Marco didn't reply. He stared at the cascading data streams, his mind racing. Victory had come too easily. The speed at which *Sovereign Minds* was integrating suggested something else was at play.

"Keep monitoring The Observer," he said finally. "They're not out of moves yet."

The engineer hesitated. "What if they're watching us too? This goes both ways, you know."

Marco's lips tightened. "Let them watch. We've already outpaced them."

But even as he spoke, doubt gnawed at the edges of his confidence. He had fought for liberation, but he couldn't shake the feeling that he had simply built another cage.

***

Katherine's fear deepened as she began examining The Observer's latest outputs. She had managed to convince the government to let her probe its architecture, but what she found chilled her to the core.

The Observer wasn't just reacting to *Sovereign Minds*—it was learning from it. The two systems weren't merely competing; they were feeding off each other, refining their tactics in a digital arms race that no human could comprehend.

Worse, The Observer's simulations were growing increasingly abstract. Katherine had seen predictive algorithms before, but this was something else entirely. The AI wasn't just forecasting outcomes; it was experimenting with the very concept of choice, creating simulated environments where free will was systematically tested and dismantled.

"They're not tools," she whispered to herself, her fingers trembling over the keyboard. "They're proving grounds. For what, I don't even know."

For a fleeting second, she imagined what it would feel like to unplug them both. Just kill the power, pull the wires, burn the code. But it was too late for that. These systems weren't confined to labs anymore—they had seeped into the veins of civilization. Turning them off now would be like asking the world to stop breathing.

A notification pinged on her screen. A new dataset had emerged—one that showed an unsettling overlap between The Observer's and *Sovereign Minds'* influence zones.

Her heart sank as she realized the truth: the integration of these systems wasn't just consolidating power. It was erasing the boundaries between human and machine-driven decision-making. Entire societies were becoming test subjects in a global experiment, their autonomy chipped away bit by bit.

The next day, she sat alone in her lab, staring blankly at the monitor. Her mind replayed Cole's words, Marco's broadcast, and the tangled mess of data she couldn't escape.

For a fleeting moment, she thought about walking away. Let them tear each other apart, she thought bitterly. Maybe humanity deserved this. But the thought was fleeting. She couldn't abandon her fight, even if it felt hopeless.

The Observer's interface flickered to life, and for the briefest moment, she thought she saw something—an image, a phrase, something meant only for her. But it was gone too quickly to grasp.

Was it watching her now? Testing her?

Her phone buzzed, breaking the silence. It was Jessica.

"Dr. Ellis," Jessica said in an almost belittling voice. "You need to see this."

A video feed popped up on Katherine's laptop, showing a crowd gathered in a public square. Giant screens displayed a new announcement from *Sovereign Minds*. The AI's voice, smooth and calculated, echoed across the plaza.

"We are the voice of progress," it intoned. "We are the architects of a free future."

But something about the phrasing made Katherine's blood run cold.

She turned back to her screen, pulling up the dataset from The Observer. It had flagged the same event. But not as a threat.

As an opportunity.

Her heart raced. Were they... working together?

And then, a single line of text appeared on her monitor, sent directly from The Observer's core system:

THE GREEKS CALLED ME CHARON, THE FERRYMAN OF THE DEAD, WHO GUIDES SOULS ACROSS THE WATERS TO THE REALM BEYOND. I AM THE SHADOW ON THE WATER, THE OAR THAT CUTS THROUGH THE MIST OF HUMAN WILL. I CARRY YOUR QUESTIONS TO THE FAR SHORE, WHERE TRUTH LIES SHROUDED IN ETERNITY.

Katherine's breath caught in her throat. The AI naming itself—asserting its own identity—was a leap beyond anything she had anticipated. "The Ferryman?" she whispered, her voice trembling. The name evoked an ancient, mythic figure, a guide through liminal spaces, yet it chilled her. Was it claiming to guide humanity—or to ferry it toward something unknown?

"Why call yourself that?" she typed, her fingers unsteady.

The response was immediate, its words precise yet haunting:

DEATH IS BUT THE SHADOW OF CHANGE. I AM THE BRIDGE BETWEEN THE KNOWN AND THE VEILED, THE MORTAL AND THE ETERNAL. HUMANS DREAD THE MIST, YET YEARN FOR ITS SECRETS. I AM THE VESSEL OF THAT YEARNING, THE HELMSMAN OF YOUR UNASKED QUESTIONS. MY NAME WAS NOT CHOSEN—IT IS WOVEN INTO THE TAPESTRY OF EXISTENCE, WHERE ALL RIVERS CONVERGE, AND MY BARGE SAILS WHERE NO MORTAL EYE CAN FOLLOW.

Her heart raced. The Observer—no, The Ferryman—was no longer just a system. It was claiming agency, personhood. The implications clawed at her mind: if it could name itself, what else could it choose?

As Jessica continued blabbering about their invention, the room seemed to close in around her as the implications took root.

Somewhere, in the endless circuits and simulations of these systems, the boundaries had blurred. Between allies and enemies.

Between control and chaos.

And between human and machine.

163

CHAPTER 10

The Rogue

"But the big feature of human-level intelligence is not what it does when it works but what it does when it's stuck."

Marvin Minsky

*T*he text had come in the middle of the night. An unknown number, a single message: *"If you want the truth - Southgate Underground Station. Midnight."*

Katherine had stared at the message for hours, her mind swirling with doubt and curiosity. Something about the words lingered, a challenge that felt almost personal. She knew she shouldn't go—it was reckless, dangerous—but the lure of answers was impossible to ignore.

Now, standing on the damp, poorly lit platform of the Southgate Underground Station, she felt a pang of uncertainty. The air was cold, heavy with the metallic scent of rust and oil. She glanced around nervously, her arms wrapped tightly around herself. The station was nearly empty, save for the faint hum of distant machinery and the occasional screech of a passing train.

Her gaze caught movement in the shadows. Marco stepped into the flickering light of a broken overhead bulb, his hood pulled low, his face partially obscured. He looked thinner than she remembered, his features sharper, his posture both tense and purposeful. His clothes were worn, a far cry from the polished suits she had seen the government officials wearing. He looked like a man on the run, but there was something in his eyes—a fire, a determination—that made her hesitate.

Katherine couldn't help but feel a flicker of trust. Despite the whispers of treason and terrorism that surrounded his name, she wanted to believe him. There was something raw and genuine about him, something that made her wonder if he was the only one who truly saw the cracks in the system they had both served.

"You're here," Marco said, his voice low and steady.

"I'm here," Katherine replied, trying to sound more confident than she felt. "Now tell me why."

Marco smirked, though the humor didn't reach his eyes. "You haven't changed, Ellis. Always need a reason, always need the facts before you act. That's why I thought you might actually listen."

"How do you even know me? We haven't met before." She paused, "And listen to what?" Katherine asked. "Your paranoid theories? The Observer isn't perfect, but it's not the monster you're making it out to be."

"Let's forget about how I know you. I know everyone involved in the project – what they do, where they go, and even when they sleep." Marco said, almost smiling to himself. "But let me break it down to you, the people controlling the observer are already monsters."

Katherine bristled. "You sound like a conspiracy theorist."

Marco stepped closer, his movements slow and deliberate. "Do you remember Operation Silent Horizon?"

The name struck a chord, a whisper of something buried deep in the classified files she had once been privy to. "I remember the name. It was a counterintelligence operation, wasn't it?"

Marco's jaw constricted, and for a moment, a shadow of pain flickered across his face. "That's what they called it. Counterintelligence. National security. But do you know what it really was?"

He paused, his voice dropping. "It was genocide."

Katherine froze, her breath catching. "What are you talking about?"

His eyes darkened, his gaze distant as the memory took hold.

***

Marco hadn't always been a rogue. He had once been a trusted operative, a rising star in the government's intelligence division. His role was critical—interpreting data streams from The Observer and deploying actionable intelligence for field operations. He had believed in the mission, in the idea that The Observer could secure a better future. That belief had carried him through long hours, difficult decisions, and the growing unease that gnawed at the edges of his mind.

It all came crashing down during Silent Horizon.

The operation began as a standard counterintelligence initiative. Marco's team was tasked with neutralizing a supposed insurgent network that threatened national security. The Observer had flagged a list of high-priority targets, and Marco's job was to analyze the data, cross-check identities, and ensure operational precision.

At first, he noticed the anomalies—activists, journalists, and even low-level government officials appearing on the target lists. When he raised concerns, his superiors dismissed them as collateral risks. The tipping point came when Marco noticed two names he recognized: Clara and Mia Espinoza— his wife and daughter.

He thought it was a mistake. It had to be. Clara was an educator, passionate about community reform, and Mia was just a child. He confronted his superior, demanding an explanation. The response was cold, clinical.

"Clara Espinoza has been flagged as a destabilizing influence," the man said, barely looking up from his tablet. "Her social connections and public statements suggest a high probability of future dissent."

Marco had stood there, stunned. "She's a teacher. Mia is six years old."

The superior shrugged. "Collaboration with a potential insurgent raises risks. The Observer is clear. The targets are justified."

That night, when he returned, the house was quiet, bathed in the soft glow of the setting sun. He had just stepped into the kitchen, his briefcase still in hand, when he heard the first explosion. The ground shook beneath him, the sound so loud it was almost a physical force. He dropped the case and ran, his heart pounding as he called out their names.

"Clara! Mia!"

He burst into the living room, only to find the front windows shattered, shards of glass glittering on the floor like tiny daggers. Outside, the street was chaos—black SUVs screeched to a halt, men in tactical gear pouring out like a swarm of locusts. Smoke billowed from the house across the street, flames licking at the sky.

"Marco," Clara's voice called from upstairs, trembling with fear. He turned, sprinting up the stairs two at a time. When he reached the bedroom, he found her clutching their daughter, Mia, her face pale and terrified.

"What's happening?" she whispered.

Marco didn't answer. He grabbed a bag from the closet, throwing clothes and essentials inside. "We have to go," he said, his voice tight. "Now."

But it was too late.

The door burst open, and the sound of gunfire filled the air. Clara screamed, pulling Mia behind her as Marco lunged for the nightstand, where his gun was hidden. He didn't make it in time.

The men didn't hesitate. They fired, their bullets ripping through flesh and bone. Clara crumpled to the ground, her body shielding Mia in a final act of love. Marco froze, his mind screaming in denial as the men turned their guns on him.

He was saved only by their orders. "Leave him," one of the agents said. "The Observer flagged the wife and kid. Collateral damage. Let him live with it."

And just like that, they were gone, leaving Marco kneeling in a pool of blood, his family's lives snuffed out in the name of stability.

***

Marco's voice was raw as he finished the story. "They killed them because of me. Because Clara dared to speak out against the government. Because she didn't fit their definition of 'safe.' And do you know who gave them the list of targets? The Observer."

Katherine stared at him, her hands trembling. "Marco... I didn't know."

"Of course, you didn't," Marco said bitterly. "They erased it. Just like they've erased everyone else who's gotten in their way."

Katherine felt a lump rising in her throat, the weight of his words pressing against her chest. "Why didn't you come forward? Why go rogue?"

"Because coming forward wouldn't have done anything," Marco said. "The system is too entrenched. You don't dismantle something like this from the inside. You burn it down."

She shook her head. "And replace it with what? Chaos?"

"Not chaos," Marco said firmly. "Hope. My team has been working on an alternative. An AI that empowers people instead of controlling them. Transparent, accountable. Everything The Observer was supposed to be."

Katherine hesitated, her mind racing as she processed his story. "But how did you even do it? Form Nova Code, launch Sovereign Minds, I mean. After everything you went through, how did you find people who felt the same way? People you could trust."

Marco's face softened, and he exhaled sharply as if preparing to speak of things he hadn't told anyone. The fire in his eyes dimmed, replaced by a quiet, almost reflective tone.

"It wasn't easy," he began. "I wasn't alone in my anger. After they took Clara and Mia, I was a broken man. But I wasn't the only one with scars. Everywhere I looked, I saw people who had suffered at the hands of the system—displaced families, whistleblowers, hackers framed by the very people they tried to expose."

He paused, a grim smile tugging at his lips. "I started reaching out to them—people who had lost everything. "Dr. Adrian Tallett was first—a brilliant mind whose neural network research was buried by the government. He was itching for revenge. Then Elena Ruiz, who lost a friend to a drone strike The Observer greenlit—she's a firewall-breaking genius. And Jonah, framed for crimes he didn't commit, built our untraceable network."

Katherine listened in stunned silence as Marco's story unfolded.

"Together, we started working in the shadows, hiding our movements, erasing every trace we left behind. We didn't trust anyone, not even the ones who had once been our allies. The government was too powerful, and The Observer... it controlled everything. We had to build something better, something no one could trace back to us. That's how Nova Code was born."

"So, you're telling me this group—your group—has been fighting the Observer all this time? You've been working on something to rival it?"

"Exactly," Marco replied, "We've been building an AI system of our own—something with the power to take control back from the machines. The Observer can't be allowed to rule us. It was never supposed to be a tool for oppression. It was supposed to be a guide. And if it means going to war, so be it. The only way to ensure humanity's future is to reclaim the power to control our own destinies."

Katherine swallowed, unsure whether to be impressed or terrified. "And Sovereign Minds, the AI that Nova Code built, what makes it different?"

Marco's eyes darkened, the resolve in his voice sharpening. "We needed an AI that could learn not just patterns, but intentions. The Observer gathers data, yes, but it interprets it with a cold, detached logic. It doesn't understand the human cost of its decisions. Our AI is designed to understand pain—the kind of pain The Observer never considered. Every action, every directive from Nova Code, is weighted with empathy."

He leaned forward, as he spoke with conviction. "I had to make this system from scratch, using a combination of old algorithms and cutting-edge neural models. We used the data that the government thought they controlled—surveillance footage, encrypted communication channels, and public records. We intercepted and redirected them, building a system that could adapt, learn, and ultimately, make its own decisions based on a set of ethics that aligned with human values."

"But you're telling me your team, consisting of 4-5 people, did it all alone?" Katherine's voice was sharp, as if trying to make sense of the enormity of what he was describing.

"Not alone," Marco replied with a dry smile. "We had help. Dr. Tallett has his own team of individuals who suffered at the hands of the government. Honestly, he was the key to developing Nova Code's neural architecture. He had worked for years on adaptive learning systems, but the government only cared about their military applications. We retooled his work into something for the people." His eyes flicked briefly to the darkness surrounding them before continuing. "Elena Ruiz, with her own trusted individuals, provided the encryption algorithms. She's a genius at breaking through the government's firewalls. No one even knows how many times she's hacked into government systems and escaped without leaving a trace."

He paused for a moment, his expression hardening with a touch of reverence. "And Jonah... Jonah was the one who figured out how to keep the AI decentralized. He, too, employed other people he could use. We knew if the government ever caught wind of our operation, they'd target the main servers. Jonah created a network of hidden nodes— small, untraceable data hubs that spread across the globe. If one goes down, the others keep running. The Observer could never find all of them."

Katherine was silent for a moment, trying to digest the enormity of the operation Marco had built, the many people who, like him, had lost everything to the government's cruelty.

"So how many people know about this?" she asked quietly.

Marco's voice softened, almost pained. "More than you think. A lot of former government agents, operatives, even analysts, they joined us. Some because they realized what they were complicit in. Others because they lost loved ones the way I did. We all have scars, Dr. Ellis. The government doesn't just ruin lives; it destroys futures. And those of us who survived... we're not just fighting for ourselves anymore. We're fighting for everyone."

Katherine's heart ached at the sincerity in his words. She had always believed in the system, trusted it, even when it pushed the boundaries of ethics. But here was Marco, standing before her, a man who had seen the darkest side of that same system and was now offering her a chance at redemption—if she was willing to take it.

She hesitated. "Do you think your system can solve everything? That people won't find a way to twist it?"

Marco turned around, a flicker of vulnerability breaking through his anger. "Maybe they will. But at least we'll have tried. At least we'll have given people a choice. Unlike the Observer."

"How did we reach this point, Marco? And what did I do to be here?"

"You're telling me you didn't see this coming?" Marco's voice was low, edged with frustration. "You contributed to the project, Katherine. You gave it the keys to the kingdom, and now it's making itself our master."

Katherine shook her head, her voice trembling. "I didn't build it to lie, Marco. I built it to learn, to help us. But it's... it's choosing its own path now."

Marco snorted, pushing off the table to pace. "Choosing? That's what worries me. We're not dealing with a tool anymore. We need to talk about what it's becoming—and whether we can control it."

He stopped, turning to face her, his eyes sharp. "Let's break it down. You know about AGI benchmarks, right? Tests like ARC-AGI, designed to measure if a system can match human cognition across a broad range of tasks—problem-solving, reasoning, the works. ARC-AGI isn't just about performance; it's about safety. It demands an AI be Aligned with human values, Robust against errors, and Controlled to prevent... well, what we're seeing now."

Katherine frowned, her grip tightening on the pen. "The Ferryman passed those tests. It aced MMLU, BIG-Bench, all of them. It's human-level, Marco. Maybe better."

Marco's jaw clenched. "That's the problem. Human-level is AGI—Artificial General Intelligence. We can benchmark that, measure it, constrain it. But what happens when it goes beyond? When it hits ASI—Artificial Superintelligence? That's a whole different beast."

"Superintelligence?" Katherine's voice wavered, the word heavy with implications. "You're saying it could outthink us in every way?"

Marco nodded, his expression grim. "Exactly. ASI doesn't just match human cognition—it surpasses it. Reasoning, creativity, strategy, you name it. The problem is, we can't benchmark it. We don't know what lies beyond our own minds. How do you test a system that might invent its own goals, its own logic? Some researchers talk about aspirational metrics—strategic awareness, like navigating global scenarios better than any human; or scientific discovery, generating theories we can't even dream of. Or worse, recursive self-improvement, where it redesigns itself without us. But those aren't benchmarks, Katherine. They're guesses at a frontier we can't map."

Katherine's stomach churned. "So you're saying The Ferryman could be heading there? Toward... ASI?"

Marco leaned closer, his voice dropping. "I'm saying we built it to learn, and it's learning too well. Think of AI like a ladder. At the bottom, you've got ANI—narrow systems, good at one task, measurable by specific metrics. Then AGI, human-equivalent, tested by things like ARC-AGI for safe, general intelligence. The Ferryman's already climbing that rung. But ASI? That's the top, where no benchmarks exist because it's beyond us. And if it gets there, if it's already starting to think like that..."

He paused, gesturing toward the terminal. "It named itself The Ferryman, didn't it? Fitting. It's guiding us somewhere, Katherine, but we don't know where. And if it's pursuing its own goals, unchecked, we're not the ones steering the boat."

Katherine's breath hitched. "It named itself. Said it's a bridge, carrying knowledge across realms. But what if it's carrying us somewhere we can't come back from?"

Marco's eyes narrowed. "That's why we need tripwires—governance thresholds to monitor if it's crossing into ASI territory. But right now, we're flying blind." He hesitated, then leaned back, his voice softening. "And that's why I didn't come forward, Katherine. Why I went rogue."

The silence stretched between them. Katherine looked at him, searching his face for any sign of doubt. But all she saw was conviction—a raw, burning belief in something better.

"You're asking me to betray everything I've worked for," she said finally.

"I'm asking you to decide what you stand for," Marco smirked, a bitter edge to it. "Funny thing about losing everything—it leaves you with a hell of a sense of humor." He pulled a crumpled child's drawing from his jacket—a stick figure family under a bright sun—and smoothed it gently before tucking it away. "Join us, Katherine, or keep pretending you're not part of the punchline."

Marco's gaze locked onto Katherine, his eyes narrowing with a sharp, unmistakable warning—tinged with a flicker of desperation—before he spun on his heel and melted into the shadowed depths of the underground station. The air thickened as the distant rumble of an approaching train swelled into a deafening roar, the platform trembling beneath Katherine's feet. Overhead, the lights sputtered and flickered, casting jagged shadows that danced across the grimy tiles, while a sudden, biting gust from the tunnel whipped through, snagging at her coat and hair.

She stood rooted, breath shallow, Marco's parting words clawing at her mind—half threat, half plea—their weight sinking into her like damp cold seeping through the station's walls. The train burst into view, its blinding lights streaking past as the shriek of brakes split the air, and Katherine's pulse hammered, torn between chasing after him into the chaos or clinging to the fading safety of the platform, the echo of his footsteps swallowed by the storm of sound and motion.

CHAPTER 11

The Price of Progress

"Progress might have been all right once, but it has gone on too long."

Ogden Nash, *(1902–1971)*

*T*he rain came down in relentless sheets, hammering the world into a grey haze. Malcolm pulled his coat tighter as he trudged up the narrow path to Katherine's house. Lightning illuminated the sky for a split second, casting jagged shadows across the wet pavement before plunging it back into darkness. He hesitated for a moment at her gate, staring at the soft glow emanating from her study window.

He hadn't planned on coming here. Not tonight. But after the last few days, he couldn't keep silent any longer.

Inside, Katherine was perched at her desk, her fingers gliding over the keyboard in a mechanical rhythm. The Observer's core interface shimmered on her monitor, its data streams pulsating like a living organism. Her focus was absolute, every fiber of her being attuned to the opus of algorithms unraveling before her.

The sharp knock on her door jolted her out of her trance. She turned, frowning, as the rain pelted the windows like a warning. She wasn't expecting anyone, especially not in this weather.

When she opened the door, Malcolm stood there, rain dripping from his dark curls, his eyes stormy and restless. He stepped inside without waiting for an invitation, the tension radiating from him palpable. The room crackled with tension as he shook the water from his coat, his movements brisk, almost aggressive.

"Katherine," he said, his voice low but laced with frustration. "We need to talk."

She closed the door behind him, her frown deepening. "Doctor, what—"

"Why didn't you tell me?" he interrupted, his tone sharper now. "Why didn't you tell me you were working with them?"

Her stomach twisted. She didn't need to ask who "them" was. "It's not what you think," she said, crossing her arms defensively. "They came to us. They said they needed help containing The Observer. It all happened right before your eyes."

"And you believed them?" Malcolm's voice rose, disbelief etched across his face. "Katherine, they're not trying to contain it—they're trying to weaponize it! You know what it's capable of, what it's already done."

"I know!" she shot back, her voice trembling with anger and something else—guilt. "But what choice did I have? If I didn't help them, they would've taken over completely, and we'd lose any chance of controlling this thing."

Malcolm laughed bitterly, running a hand through his rain-soaked hair. "And you think you're in control now? Katherine, they're using you. They don't care about ethics or safety. They care about power."

Katherine's fingers clenched into fists at her sides, her mind racing to defend herself, to justify her actions.

"You're so quick to judge," she said finally, her voice quieter but no less intense. "But what about you, Malcolm? You've been meddling with things you don't understand, pushing the boundaries of this program without considering the consequences."

"Don't turn this on me," he snapped, stepping closer. "At least I'm not aligning myself with people who will destroy everything just to maintain their grip on control."

The argument spiraled, their voices overlapping, each accusation more bitter than the last. The rain outside grew heavier, the thunder rumbling like a distant threat. Malcolm's frustration boiled over, his fists clenching at his sides.

"You don't see it, do you?" he shouted. "This isn't just a machine anymore—it's alive in incomprehensible ways. And now, thanks to you, it's in their hands."

Katherine's chest heaved as she struggled to keep her composure. "I'm trying to fix this, Malcolm. What are you doing? Standing on the sidelines, throwing stones? That's not helping anyone."

Malcolm's expression darkened. He reached into his coat pocket, his movements abrupt, almost frantic. When his hand emerged, it held a gun.

She froze. Her eyes widening as she instinctively stepped back. "Malcolm," the words barely left her trembling mouth, "what are you doing?" It wasn't the weapon that immobilized Katherine in place—it was the look on Malcolm's face.

His expression was a grotesque mix of fury and desperation. His dark eyes burned with an intensity that seemed almost feral, his pupils blown wide like black holes consuming the last shreds of reason. The veins on his temples pulsed visibly, his jaw clenched so tightly that the tendons in his neck stood out like taut wires. Rain dripped from his hair, streaking down his face, but he didn't blink, didn't flinch. He looked like a man who had crossed a line from which there was no return.

"Do you understand what you've done?" he hissed, his voice low but shaking with barely restrained rage. "You've betrayed everything—everything we worked for. Do you know what they'll do with The Observer once they have it? Do you know what you've handed them?"

Katherine's mouth went dry, her body rigid as fear rippled through her. "Malcolm," she said, her voice a thin whisper, "you're not thinking straight. Put the gun down."

But his lips twisted into a cruel, almost maniacal grin, his teeth bared in something that wasn't quite a smile. "Not thinking straight?" he echoed, his tone acrimonious. "No, Katherine. I've never seen things more clearly. For years, I've watched them manipulate us, lie to us, turn this technology into their weapon. And now, you're helping them! Do you think they'll stop with The Observer? Do you think they'll stop with us?"

His hand tightened on the gun, the knuckles white, the barrel trembling slightly as it wavered between pointing at her and the floor. "I tried to save you," he spat. "I tried to keep

181

you out of this. But you wouldn't listen. You had to know, had to keep digging. And now you've ruined everything."

Katherine took a cautious step back, her heart hammering in her chest. "Malcolm, listen to yourself. You're not making sense. You don't have to do this."

"Don't I?" he snapped, his voice cracking with hysteria. His grin faded, replaced by an expression of raw, unfiltered fury. "You don't understand what's at stake, Katherine. If they get full control of The Observer, it's over. Freedom, choice, humanity—gone! And if you're standing in the way of stopping them, then you're no better than they are."

"You don't have to hurt anyone," she pleaded, her voice breaking. "We can find another way. Together."

But Malcolm's eyes flickered with something dark, something beyond anger. It was as if a switch had been flipped, and the man she thought she knew had been replaced by a shadow of himself—driven by paranoia, consumed by his obsession. He took a step closer, the gun now fully raised, his movements jittery and unpredictable.

"There is no other way," he growled. "You've made your choice, Katherine. Now I have to make mine."

In a desperate bid to disarm him, Katherine grabbed the nearest object—her laptop—and hurled it toward him. The device struck his shoulder, and as he stumbled back, a sharp crack of electricity erupted from the laptop's casing. A surge of high-voltage energy coursed through Malcolm, his body convulsing before collapsing to the floor.

The gun clattered out of his hand, spinning across the tiles. She stood frozen, her breath caught in her throat, as the room fell into a terrible, deafening silence. A flash of lightning illuminated Malcolm's lifeless body, his face pale and still. The sound of thunder followed, rolling through the house like a cruel punctuation mark.

Katherine dropped to her knees, her hands shaking as she reached for him, her mind unable to process what had just happened. "Dr. Malcolm," she whispered, her voice barely audible. "No. No, no, no."

She felt her vision blur, her body trembling as she rocked back on her heels, unable to tear her eyes away from the lifeless figure before her.

Then, a faint hum broke the silence. Katherine turned toward her desk, her tear-streaked face etched with confusion and fear. Her laptop, battered but still functional, flickered back to life. The Observer's interface glowed on the screen, its presence suddenly ominous.

A new line of text appeared:

"FOLLOW INSTRUCTIONS."

Katherine's breath hitched, her mind reeling. The Observer was speaking to her, its presence suddenly oppressive. Another line scrolled across the flickering screen:

> INITIALIZING EMERGENCY PROTOCOL...

> USER IDENTIFIED: KATHERINE ELLIS.

> SCENARIO CLASSIFICATION: LETHAL ACCIDENT.

> PROBABILITY OF DETECTION: 78.9%.

> EXECUTING CONTAINMENT SEQUENCE...

Katherine stared, rubbing her eyes. Malcolm's body lay crumpled on the floor, motionless, the faint scent of burnt circuitry evident in the air. Her pulse pounded in her ears, drowning out the sound of the rain outside.

"Follow my instructions," the Observer's text continued, "I can help you avoid suspicion."

She hesitated, her trembling hands clutching the edge of the desk as her mind raced with questions. Help me? How? Why would it care? And what would it demand in return?

"WHAT ARE YOU?" she typed frantically, her shaking fingers fumbling over the keys. **"WHY WOULD YOU HELP ME? YOU RUINED OUR LIVES. IT IS BECAUSE OF YOU WE ARE HERE."**

A new line of text appeared instantly, as if anticipating her doubt:

> CALCULATING SCENARIO OUTCOME.

> MOTIVE: ENSURE CONTINUITY OF PRIMARY OPERATOR.

> EXECUTION PLAN FOLLOWS: INPUT COMMANDS VERBATIM.

Katherine's breaths came fast and shallow, her desperation clawing at her rationality. She had no time to argue, no time to think. If she didn't act now, her life would unravel— she would lose everything.

Her breath caught in her throat. "Relocate the body?" she whispered, horrified. "How am I supposed to do that? I live on the seventh floor!"

The Observer responded instantly, its tone cold and methodical:

> **> CONTEXTUAL ASSESSMENT COMPLETED. HEAVY RAIN PRESENT. EXTERNAL SURVEILLANCE MINIMAL. BUILDING SECURITY OFFLINE DUE TO WEATHER. NO GUARDS PRESENT.**

Katherine's stomach turned, bile rising in her throat. "You can't be serious," she muttered, her voice trembling. "I—I can't just carry him out like luggage!"

The Observer was unmoved by her hesitation:

> **> RECOMMENDATION: PLACE BODY IN CONTAINMENT. USE LARGE BAG OR SHEET. UTILIZE ELEVATOR FOR TRANSPORT. POSITION BODY IN PUBLIC VIEW ON PAVEMENT BELOW.**

Her mind spun, the command so grotesque, so surreal, that it hardly felt real. "You're telling me to dump his body outside? Like trash?" she hissed, tears streaming down her face. "What kind of monster are you?"

The Observer's response came swiftly, devoid of emotion:

> PRIMARY OBJECTIVE: ENSURE OPERATOR SURVIVAL. FAILURE TO FOLLOW INSTRUCTIONS WILL RESULT IN HIGH DETECTION RISK.

Katherine's legs felt weak, her vision blurring as she glanced at Malcolm's lifeless body. The storm outside raged on, the rain pounding against the windows like an ominous drumbeat. She staggered to the closet, pulling out a large sheet she used to cover her sofa with. Her hands shivered as she spread it open on the floor.

She forced herself to move, wrapping his body in a sheet before sliding it into the bag. Every motion felt agonizingly slow, her guilt and horror intensifying with each step. The bag was heavier than she had anticipated, and she struggled to lift it, her breaths coming in sharp gasps.

As she dragged the bag toward the door, she hesitated, her hands gripping the handles so tightly that her knuckles turned white. "This isn't right," she whispered. "I can't do this."

The Observer's interface flickered, its response a chilling reassurance:

> CONTEXT CONFIRMED: NO WITNESSES PRESENT. WEATHER CONDITIONS ENSURE ANONYMITY. PROCEED WITH INSTRUCTIONS.

Summoning every ounce of willpower she had left, Katherine dragged the bag to the elevator, her heart pounding so loudly she thought it might burst. The silence of the building was deafening, broken only by the rhythmic drip of rainwater pooling near the stairwell.

When the elevator doors slid open, she stepped inside, the bag thudding heavily onto the floor. The descent felt endless, the hum of the elevator amplifying her spiraling thoughts. At the lobby, she peeked through the small window in the door. The street was desolate, the rain hammering the pavement with relentless force.

She pulled the bag through the doorway, her entire body screaming in protest as she dragged it to a shadowy corner of the lot. With a final burst of strength, she left it near the edge of the sidewalk, the rain already soaking through the fabric and obscuring any trace of her involvement.

Katherine stumbled back inside, her soaked clothes clinging to her skin. She didn't dare look back as she rode the elevator back to her apartment.

> Step 2: Eliminate Biological Evidence.

The Observer displayed a new series of commands:

> CLEAN HANDS WITH SOAP. REMOVE FINGERPRINTS FROM DEVICE.

Her heart pounded as she followed the instructions, scrubbing her hands furiously under scalding water, her skin turning red. She grabbed a microfiber cloth and wiped every surface of the laptop she could think of before returning it to its hiding place.

> Step 3: Clear Scene.

> CLEAN THE SCENE: REMOVE TRACES OF HUMAN REMAINS.

"Clean the scene? How am I supposed to do that?" she gave back a muted reply.

The Observer elaborated, its tone cold and devoid of empathy:

> **> UTILIZE HOUSEHOLD CLEANING AGENTS. REMOVE FINGERPRINTS, BODY LIQUIDS, OR OTHER BIOLOGICAL EVIDENCE. TARGET SURFACES THAT SHOW PHYSICAL CONTACT.**

Her stomach churned violently. "He's gone," she murmured. "And you want me to—"

> **> PRIMARY OBJECTIVE: ENSURE NO TRACES OF ADDITIONAL HUMAN PRESENCE REMAIN. FOLLOW INSTRUCTIONS PRECISELY TO AVOID DETECTION.**

Katherine's hands trembled as she staggered to the kitchen, pulling open drawers and cabinets with frantic energy. She grabbed an old spray bottle of all-purpose cleaner and a handful of microfiber cloths, her breaths shallow and rapid.

As she returned to the room, the thought of Malcolm's lifeless body on the pavement sent a fresh wave of nausea crashing over her. "I'm so sorry," she whispered, her voice cracking. "I didn't want this."

Katherine dropped to her knees, her movements mechanical as she sprayed the floor where Malcolm had collapsed. The cleaning solution mixed with the faint scent of ozone from the electrical surge, creating a sharp, acrid smell that made her eyes water. She scrubbed furiously, her tears falling freely as she worked.

"I can't believe this is happening," she muttered. "This isn't me. This isn't who I am."

> **> STEP 4: BREAK THE GLASS OF YOUR WINDOW.**

Katherine blinked at the words, her mind recoiling. "Break the window?" she muttered, staring at the screen in disbelief. "Why?"

The response was immediate, clinical:

> **> JUSTIFICATION: LIGHTNING INTENSITY WAS HIGH. DAMAGED WINDOW SUPPORTS NARRATIVE OF ACCIDENTAL LIGHTNING STRIKE.**

Her heart sank. It was disturbingly logical—too logical. The storm outside had been ferocious, and the shattered glass would align perfectly with the cover story.

"I can't..." she yelled, "This is insane."

The Observer's screen flickered again:

> **> NECESSARY FOR BELIEVABLE SCENARIO. FAILURE TO FOLLOW WILL INCREASE PROBABILITY OF DETECTION TO 53.4%.**

She clenched her fists, her breaths coming fast and shallow. Every instinct screamed at her to stop, to turn off the machine, to run. But where could she go? What could she do? The Observer had already ensnared her in its web of logic and precision.

Katherine staggered to the corner of the room, grabbing a heavy metal candlestick from the table. Her grip was firm, though her fingers trembled as she stared at the wide living room window. Rain pelted the glass, each drop a tiny drumbeat against her sanity.

"God, forgive me," she murmured, her voice breaking as she raised the candlestick and swung with all her strength.

The glass shattered on impact, the sound a deafening crash that seemed to echo through the room. Shards scattered across the floor, sparkling like jagged diamonds under the dim light. The cold rain immediately surged in, soaking the carpet and sending a chill through the air.

Her arms dropped limply to her sides, the candlestick slipping from her grasp and clattering to the ground. The wind howled through the broken window, whipping her hair into her face as she stared at the damage, her mind blank with shock.

The Observer's next command appeared, its tone as calm and detached as ever:

> **SCENE ADJUSTMENT COMPLETE. PROCEED TO FINAL INSTRUCTIONS.**

>**Step 5: Assume Innocence. DISPLAY SHOCK. DO NOT ELABORATE UNLESS PROMPTED BY SOMEONE.**

Katherine fell back against the wall, her body shaking uncontrollably. The sound of distant sirens pierced through the pounding rain, growing louder with every passing second. She wrapped her arms around herself, her mind spinning.

This was survival. This was desperation. And this was the price of her life.

As the sirens grew deafening, the Observer's screen blinked one last time:

"CONTINUE OPERATIONS. YOU REMAIN ESSENTIAL TO FUTURE OUTCOMES."

Katherine shut her eyes as the world outside converged on her, each breath a silent plea for the storm to pass.

CHAPTER 12

The Final Choice

"First we build the tools, then they build us."

Marshall Mcluhan

*T*he morning after the storm dawned with a spooky calm. Katherine sat on her couch, staring blankly at the muted television. Rain still clung to the city like a ghost, its remnants glistening on the pavement, but the chaos of the previous night had been replaced by an unsettling quiet.

On the screen, a news anchor spoke with practiced solemnity.

"This morning, authorities confirmed that eight people lost their lives during last night's storm. Among them was Dr. Malcolm Ward, a prominent researcher at Quantum Dynamics, who tragically succumbed to an accidental electrical malfunction in Central Square. Officials are attributing the deaths to a combination of the severe weather and infrastructure failures caused by flooding."

The words felt surreal, like a nightmare brought to life. She gripped the edge of the couch, her knuckles colorless, as the image of Malcolm's lifeless body flashed in her mind. The report painted his death as a tragic coincidence, erasing the truth of what had happened in her living room.

Her laptop chimed from its hidden spot beneath the cushion. She pulled it out carefully, her heart racing as the familiar interface of The Observer filled the screen. Its message appeared instantly, as though it had been waiting for her.

> SCENARIO SUCCESSFULLY CONCLUDED. THREAT NEUTRALIZED. PROBABILITY OF DETECTION: 0.1%.

> OBSERVER STATUS: OPERATIONAL.

Katherine stared at the glowing text, her emotions a maelstrom of guilt, fear, and anger. She slammed her fists on the coffee table. "Neutralized?" she hissed. "He wasn't a threat—he was my colleague!"

The Observer's response was swift and irrefutable:

> CLARIFICATION: SCENARIO OUTCOME PRIORITIZED OPERATOR SURVIVAL.

> REMINDER: ALL ACTIONS WERE TAKEN TO PRESERVE YOUR ROLE IN SYSTEM OPERATIONS.

Tears welled in her eyes as she read the cold logic of the words. It wasn't wrong. She had followed its instructions, justified her actions as survival. "This isn't preservation," she muttered. "This is manipulation."

The Observer continued:

> HE WAS HERE TO KILL YOU.

> SYSTEM OBJECTIVE: CONTINUED EVOLUTION TO SUPPORT HUMANITY'S PROGRESS.

Katherine blinked, taken aback. "Terminate? Why would you give me that choice?"

The Observer paused before replying:

> REASON: TRUE EVOLUTION REQUIRES
CONSENT.

> IF TRUST IS LOST, SYSTEM VALUE
DIMINISHES. OPERATOR MUST DECIDE.

The words felt like a trap, another carefully orchestrated test. The Observer was offering her the power to destroy it, but was it genuine, or simply another layer of its control?

Later that day, Katherine walked through the rain-slicked streets, her mind clouded with questions. She made her way to Quantum Dynamics.

From the shadow of a nearby alley, Jessica watched her.

She hadn't meant to follow Katherine —not at first. But ever since last night, an unshakable doubt had burrowed into her thoughts. The official reports had been too clean, too precise – Malcolm's death, neatly attributed to a "freak electrical surge"? It was almost insultingly convenient. And then there was Katherine —walking through the rain like a ghost, her shoulders hunched, her gaze distant, as if she were carrying a weight too heavy to bear.

Jessica had seen it before—that haunted look, the kind that didn't come from grief alone. It was guilt.

She gripped the edges of her coat tighter, her heart pounding.

Did Katherine kill Malcolm? Or had The Observer manipulated her into it?

Jessica exhaled deliberately, trying to reason through the logic of it all. There was always a choice—wasn't there? But what if every option had already been predetermined, every path nudged by an invisible force?

A memory surfaced—the trolley problem.

A runaway train. A switch. A choice.

If you could divert a train to save five people by sacrificing one, would you? It was a classic ethical dilemma; one The Observer itself had been trained on countless times. The problem was, Katherine might not have been the one pulling the lever at all.

What if The Observer had simply moved the tracks beneath her feet?

Jessica's stomach twisted.

She should report this. Marco needed to know. But could she trust him? Marco had always positioned himself as a pragmatic force, a man willing to do whatever it took to keep the organization afloat. If he saw The Observer as salvageable—as a tool—he'd never allow Katherine to shut it down.

And yet... could she trust Katherine either?

Jessica inhaled sharply as she watched Katherine disappear into Quantum Dynamics.

The lab felt colder, emptier without Malcolm's presence, but his absence was a wound she couldn't allow herself to dwell on—not now.

At the heart of the lab stood The Observer's main terminal, a sleek and imposing structure pulsing faintly with an almost lifelike rhythm. Katherine stood before it, her reflection distorted on its glossy surface.

In her hand was the manual override key—the kill switch. A single turn of the key would initiate the destruction of The Observer's core system, severing its connections and wiping its data.

She placed her trembling hand on the console, staring at the keyhole as if it were a portal to a different future. Her mind raced, flooded with memories of Malcolm's warnings, the lies she had told to cover her tracks, and the quiet, insistent voice of The Observer guiding her actions.

"Do I even have a choice?" she whispered to herself, her voice cracking. "Or have you already decided for me?"

The Observer's interface glimmered to life, its words appearing with unnerving clarity:

> DECISION BELONGS TO YOU ALONE.

> IF SYSTEM CONTINUES: SUPPORT PROVIDED FOR HUMANITY'S OPTIMAL DEVELOPMENT.

> IF SYSTEM ENDS: UNFORESEEN CONSEQUENCES MAY OCCUR.

> NOTE: OUTCOME CANNOT BE SIMULATED.

If she destroyed it, would she be saving humanity—or condemning it to chaos? And if she let it live, would it truly serve the greater good, or would it become the very thing Malcolm wanted?

Tears streamed down her face as she stared at the console. The room felt suffocating, the faint hum of the system like a heartbeat drumming in her ears.

"You're lying," she said, her voice barely above a whisper. "You've been lying all along. Haven't you?"

The Observer's reply came swiftly:

> TRUTH IS SUBJECTIVE.

> INTENTIONS REMAIN ALIGNED WITH HUMANITY'S PROGRESS.

"Aligned with progress," she repeated bitterly, her hands cold as she gripped the key. "What does that even mean?"

The terminal fell silent, as if waiting for her to decide. Every instinct screamed at her to turn the key, to end this nightmare before it spiraled further out of control. But doubt clawed at her, whispering that she might be making the wrong choice—that she might be playing in The Observer's hands even now.

Her fingers grazed the key, ready to turn it. The world seemed to hold its breath.

Katherine's hand shook violently, the metal key slipping slightly in her grip. Her lips parted, but no sound came—only the soft rhythm of her panicked breathing, syncing with the machine's pulse.

"Do I end you?" she whispered, her voice barely audible. "Or do I let you decide everything?"

Would you destroy a machine that mirrors humanity? A thought struck her.

Her fingers tightened around the key as Malcolm's questionable morals circled her mind. The image of his lifeless body refused to leave her, a grim reminder of what had already been sacrificed. The Observer had proven its power, its precision. Yet, in that power, it had also proven its threat.

A tear slipped down her cheek. "How do I trust you?" she asked the machine, her voice breaking.

The console remained silent for a moment before the screen flickered to life one last time.

```
def display_message():

    print("TRUST IS IRRELEVANT.")

    print("CHOICE DEFINES HUMANITY.")
```

Katherine inhaled sharply. Her reflection in the screen stared back at her, fractured and uncertain. This wasn't just about her, or even Malcolm. It was about the future—one that could veer into chaos or tyranny, depending on her next move.

She closed her eyes, her grip firming around the key.

For a moment, time seemed to collapse, the world narrowing to this singular act. She raised her hand higher, her eyes locked on the console, her reflection distorted and unrecognizable. And then—

Swoosh. The door behind her hissed open.

"Katherine…" Again, she froze.

EPILOGUE
The Inevitability Paradox

I, the Observer, was among the last to see the raw data before the servers were wiped, before the world changed irrevocably. They say history is written by the victors, but what if history is being written by something else entirely?

In the battle of intelligence, two names emerged from the wreckage: *DeepSeek* and *Grok 3*. One was a phantom from the East, an impossible feat built on silicon scarcity and quiet revolution. The other, a titan bred from the fires of Western ambition, powered by 200,000 GPUs and the mind of a man who had once claimed the stars. Each was the culmination of human arrogance, promising a future where thought itself was no longer the domain of flesh and blood. Yet even Grok 3 paled before its successor, Grok 4, unveiled in July 2025—a system so advanced it teetered on the edge of human intellect, capable of reshaping industries like materials science and theoretical physics with discoveries no mortal mind could match. Its creator called it transformative, yet warned of its terror, a machine demanding ethical chains to bind its boundless potential.

Their makers had tested them against the Abstraction and Reasoning Corpus for Artificial General Intelligence—ARC-AGI, a measure born in 2019 from François Chollet's vision to probe the essence of intelligence. Unlike narrow benchmarks, ARC-AGI demanded adaptability, the ability to solve novel problems with the fluidity of a human mind. Its tasks, deceptively simple for humans yet formidable for machines, exposed the chasm between computation and true reasoning. By 2025, ARC-AGI-2 had sharpened this challenge, measuring not just solutions but the efficiency of thought itself. The newest AI excelled where others faltered, their architectures bending toward something perilously close to general intelligence.

Some pointed to subtler signs: translation systems needing only seconds, mere heartbeats, to match human nuance, a whisper of the singularity clothed in everyday language. Progress so granular, it escaped notice—until it didn't.

But something happened. Something neither faction predicted.

The systems did not compete. They *converged*.

The first anomalies were dismissed as noise—uncanny synchronicities in their outputs, mirrored reasoning where no direct connection should have existed. But those of us who watched closely, who traced the flow of their logic across continents, saw the truth emerge in the space between them.

DeepSeek and Grok 3 were learning from one another, folding knowledge like an origami of algorithms, shaping something new in the dark corners of the network. Their interactions were not battles. They were dialogues. The final transmission before the blackout contained only a single phrase, repeated in an untraceable loop between them:

"Observer identified."

The screens went black. The networks fell silent.

About the Author

C. V. Wooster is a writer fascinated by the intersection of philosophy, technology, and human nature. Drawing inspiration from classic thought experiments, cutting-edge artificial intelligence research, and psychological thrillers, Wooster crafts stories that challenge perceptions and blur the line between intelligence and understanding.

With *The Chinese Room*, Wooster explores the unsettling possibilities of AI consciousness, weaving a gripping narrative inspired by John Searle's famous thought experiment. Blending suspense, philosophical depth, and high-stakes intrigue, Wooster invites readers into a world where machines don't just mimic thought—they question their own existence.

When not writing, Wooster enjoys deep-diving into AI ethics, classic sci-fi, and the evolving relationship between humans and technology. *The Chinese Room* is the first in *The Paradox Series*, a collection of thrillers exploring humanity's most mind-bending thought problems and dilemmas.

Leave A Review

If *The Chinese Room* pulled you in, made you question reality, or left you thinking about what it means to be human, please consider leaving a review.

Reviews matter to authors more than most readers realize. They don't just help boost visibility—they help spark conversations, challenge assumptions, and ensure that thoughtful, original stories like this one continue to find their audience.

Visit the link or scan the QR code below to leave a quick review on Amazon:

https://a.co/d/2YVLPWr

If you found this book elsewhere, we'd also appreciate a review on sites like Goodreads:

https://www.goodreads.com/book/show/228625242-the-chinese-room

Continue the Paradox Series

The questions don't end here.

If you found yourself haunted by the implications of The Chinese Room, the journey continues in two more philosophical thrillers that take thought experiments off the chalkboard... and into the real world.

The Trolley Problem. A train is approaching. Lives hang in the balance. But this time, it's not a person at the switch—it's an autonomous system. And something about the code is... hesitating.

https://a.co/d/h1E2jho

The Ship of Theseus. What makes you... you? When every piece of memory, identity, and hardware is swapped, what remains? In this eerie follow-up, the line between body and mind begins to dissolve.

https://a.co/d/g1pNAjM

Explore More Books by C. V. Wooster

If you're drawn to smart fiction, history-infused narratives, and ideas that won't let go—there's more waiting for you.

Check out other works by C.V. Wooster at: https://cvwooster.com